ANNIE'S ATTIC MYSTERIES®

The Kennel Caper

Jan Fields

Annie's®

AnniesMysteries.com

Books in the Annie's Attic Mysteries series

Library of Congress-in-Publication Data
The Kennel Caper / by Jan Fields
p. cm.
I. Title
                    2013904570

AnniesMysteries.com
800-282-6643
Annie's Attic Mysteries®
Series Editors: Ken and Janice Tate
Series Creator: Stenhouse & Associates, Ridgefield, Connecticut
Photography: Cover image by Gina Callaway/Shutterstock.com.

10 11 12 13 14 | Printed in China | 9 8 7 6

— 1 —

nnie Dawson hitched the wire handles on the basket
higher up on her forearm as she wandered around
the produce section at Magruder's Grocery.
Compared to the huge supermarket where she shopped
in Texas, the little grocery store was cozy but not as well
lighted. On the plus side, Magruder's carried local produce
all summer, and Annie loved the freshness. She'd already
slipped some beautiful dark red tomatoes into her basket for
her favorite summer treat—tomato sandwiches. Some pest
had sheared off the blooms of her own tomato plants, so she
had to rely on Magruder's for the fruit.

She sighed as she turned, scanning the shelves and
waiting for inspiration to hit her. It was early Sunday afternoon; normally Annie didn't have to worry about lunch
and dinner plans after church, but she had gotten into a
bit of a cooking funk. She thought about how challenging
meal preparation had seemed back when she was a young
mother, trying to choose something for supper that would
suit both her hard-working husband, Wayne, and a mildly
picky little girl. Her daughter LeeAnn had grown up to be a
very adventurous eater, but now LeeAnn's twins—John and
Joanna—sometimes drove their mom crazy with their own
dueling pickiness. Annie smiled at the passing thought of
her only grandchildren.

Now Annie welcomed the challenge of cooking for others whenever she had a party or contributed to a community event, but cooking just for herself seemed dull. Too often she settled on canned soup and sandwiches because they were easy. *Maybe I should invite Ian over for supper one day this week*, she thought. *That might inspire a little culinary creativity again.*

Ian Butler, the gregarious mayor of Annie's adoptive town of Stony Point, Maine, had in the past several years grown to be Annie's love interest. It had been a long struggle to get emotionally and psychologically past her husband Wayne's death from a sudden, massive heart attack, but Annie had finally reached a peaceful place in her soul that allowed her to invite Ian into her heart.

"Annie!"

Annie looked up to find Kate Stevens walking up the aisle, her daughter Vanessa trailing behind. The teen's eyes were intent on the phone in her hands, although every now and then she looked up and around as if hoping to find herself somewhere besides a grocery store. Annie smiled at Vanessa's perfect look of teen boredom, from her slightly dragging sneakers to the occasional pained groan. She remembered how much LeeAnn had complained about being forced to enter the grocery store for any reason when she was that age.

"You looking for Sunday dinner inspiration too?" Annie asked.

Kate shook her head. "We're buying supplies for the youth bake sale at church." Her eyes flashed toward Vanessa. "You know, the one I only just heard about."

Vanessa looked up from her phone and shrugged. "I forgot."

"I could bake something," Annie offered. "When is the bake sale?"

"They're setting up a booth at the farmers market on Tuesday afternoon," Kate said. "If you want to make something and give it to me at the Hook and Needle Club Meeting on Tuesday, that would be great." Kate, a fellow member of the handcraft club, also worked at A Stitch in Time, Stony Point's needle-art shop.

"Sure, I was just hoping to have some inspiration for cooking."

"I know that feeling," Kate agreed.

Vanessa frowned and harrumphed at her phone before shoving it into her purse. She looked up almost as if she'd spotted Annie for the first time. She smiled, and Annie saw a flash of Kate's warmth in Vanessa's smile. "Logan says hi," she said.

Annie looked at the girl in surprise. Logan Lariby was a young actor who had taken quite a fancy to Vanessa when he was in town making a movie sometime back. Annie liked the actor. He'd been a huge help in solving a mystery surrounding an old valise, a mystery that had taken a scary turn. "You two keep in touch?" she asked.

"Yes, though it was mostly just email until this summer," Vanessa said, her eyes sparkled with excitement as she spoke. "He's in a play on Broadway, and he texts me about everything. I almost feel like I'm in the show! Mom said we could go to the city to see it."

"Might!" Kate said. "I told you we *might* go."

"Logan is sending tickets and backstage passes," Vanessa said. "It'll be great to see him."

"Great," Kate echoed, though she sounded less enthusiastic. Annie could understand that. Logan was a nice guy, polite and good-hearted, but Annie wouldn't have been thrilled to have her teenage daughter involved with an actor either. They weren't really known for their stability.

Annie wasn't surprised when Kate changed the subject. "What do you think of these break-ins?"

"I think it's good that Reverend Wallace reminded everyone to be careful and lock their doors," Annie said. "He struck the right tone of caution without scaring people."

"I have to admit, I'm a little scared," Kate said.

"Well, it sounds like all the break-ins were when people were out of town," Annie said.

"Which is exactly what we'll be if we go to that Broadway play," Kate reminded her. "I don't like to leave our home vacant. We don't own a lot of things that would interest a thief, but I still don't want to take any chances."

Annie nodded. She wasn't a wealthy woman either, but her home—Grey Gables—had been broken into more than once since she moved to Stony Point from her native Texas. The feeling of violation was terrifying every single time. It was the sort of thing she really wasn't likely to get used to. Of course, all of her break-ins were directly related to mysteries Annie was investigating in one way or another. However, that didn't make the break-ins any less scary.

Vanessa crossed her arms. "You just don't want me to see Logan."

"That's not it," Kate said. "You know that I like Logan."

"Sure," Vanessa said. "I'm going out to wait in the car. I get terrible reception in here. Anything you want to buy for the bake sale is fine." She turned and stomped down the aisle.

Kate watched her daughter storm away. She looked at Annie with a sad smile. "I don't remember being that sullen when I was a teenager."

"Vanessa won't remember being that sullen either," Annie said. "She'll just remember being misunderstood."

Kate laughed lightly. "That I do remember. I guess you're right. I don't really mind Vanessa seeing Logan. He's a sweet guy, and they seem to be keeping it on a friendship level. I really don't like the idea of leaving town right now with the break-ins. Peggy told me that Chief Edwards is sure the thieves are casing the homes. I hate the thought of some criminal sizing up my house for a robbery."

"I'm sure Chief Edwards will track down whoever is doing this," Annie said.

"Peggy said he doesn't have any leads," Kate told her.

Annie shook her head. "Sounds like Peggy has been lingering near tables again." As a waitress at The Cup & Saucer, Peggy Carson had access to the perfect information stream. Everyone in Stony Point ate at the little diner since the food was great and the atmosphere was homey. That meant that Peggy knew almost everything about almost everyone, and she didn't mind sharing it. Keeping a secret in Stony Point was almost impossible.

"Peggy means well," Kate said, "and I like knowing how the investigation is going. That way I know exactly how much to worry."

"I do think we all need to be careful, but I don't know that we really need to worry. Weren't all three of the homes robbed so far big and fancy?"

"Well, yes," Kate said.

"It sounds like the thieves are interested in places where they can get the most valuables," Annie said. "If they're casing the places as Chief Edwards thinks, I expect they're not really looking at the more modest homes."

"That does make sense," Kate said. "My house is tiny."

"I wonder if the victims have anything else in common besides big houses," Annie said.

"Well, they were all out of town at the time of the robberies," Kate said. "You know, you might be right about *my* house being safe, but *you* probably shouldn't go out of town. Since you've put all the time and attention into Grey Gables, it looks really nice."

Annie looked at her friend in surprise. Grey Gables was a beautiful old Victorian-era home that Annie had inherited from her dearly loved grandmother, Elizabeth Holden, but Annie definitely didn't think of it as fancy. "You really think so?"

"I know that most of the beautiful, old restored homes around Stony Point belong to families with money," Kate said.

"Wayne left me comfortable enough," Annie said, "but I'm far from wealthy. If I hadn't done part of the work myself, and if Wally hadn't given me such a good deal on all the work he did—I'd still have roof leaks and mouse nests." Peggy's husband, Wally, was a skilled handyman with an amazing eye for detail.

"I know that," Kate said. "But do the burglars know that?" Kate looked at Annie with concern. "I'm sorry, now I'm passing my paranoia onto you. They've probably not given Grey Gables a single thought."

Maybe not, Annie thought. She'd had more than enough break-ins at Grey Gables. Maybe this time she needed to look into the mystery of how to keep the bad guys *out* of her house.

~ 2 ~

"You know," Annie said, "maybe these break-ins are something the Hook and Needle Club should talk about at our next meeting."

"Talk about?" Kate echoed. Then her face broke into a grin. "You mean as a mystery?"

"Well, it sounds like Peggy is already on the job," Annie said. "Of course, I'm sure Stella won't approve."

Stella Brickson, the regal octogenarian, saw herself as the matriarch of their group and often chided them for being more interested in mysteries than needlework. That being said, once the mysteries were underway, Stella was as apt as anyone else to take part. She'd never admit it, but Annie knew she loved the excitement.

"You know Mary Beth will love it," Kate said.

Mary Beth Brock was the owner of A Stitch in Time, the needlecraft shop where the club meetings took place. She had every bit as much natural curiosity as Peggy, and the two of them could be counted on to know everything about everyone around Stony Point. Annie was sure the club would find a new mystery exciting.

"I don't want to get in the way of a real police investigation," Annie said. "But I don't like this happening right here in … in … *achoo!*" Annie sneezed sharply into the crook of her arm. Then she sneezed twice more right after.

"Bless you," Kate said. "You sound like me around cats. Is something triggering an allergy?"

Annie shook her head. "I don't really have allergies, especially this time of year." she answered, her voice already sounded a little stuffed. Then she sneezed three more times. She felt burning in her nose, and the back of her throat ached slightly. "I hope I'm not coming down with something."

Kate looked at her with sympathy. "Summer colds are the worst. Maybe it was just dust in here."

Annie nodded, though she knew Mike Magruder kept the store very clean. She quickly slipped a couple cans of soup into her basket, just in case she was catching a cold. "I think I better finish up here and get home. I don't want to spread my germs around if I am coming down with something."

Kate nodded. "Call me if you need anything."

"Thanks. I'm sure I'll see you Tuesday at the Hook and Needle Club meeting, and I'll bring something for Vanessa's bake sale."

Annie hurried down the aisle, suddenly eager to get home. By the time she pulled into the driveway at Grey Gables, she already felt achy and hot.

As she carried the bag of groceries into the house, Annie's gray cat, Boots, rushed to greet her. Annie had inherited the intrepid feline along with Grey Gables. Annie began to sneeze a rapid-fire series of mini-explosions. Boots flattened her ears and backed away on her white-tipped paws.

"Sorry, Boots," Annie said. "I think I've caught a cold."

Even to Annie's ears, her voice sounded rough. Boots definitely didn't like the strange sounds coming from Annie. The cat puffed up before turning and dashing down the hall toward the kitchen.

Annie carried the groceries into the kitchen, but she didn't see the cat. She put everything away and put the kettle on the stove for tea. She kept expecting Boots to overcome her fright and march into the kitchen, meowing for a snack. It certainly wasn't like the cat to let Annie brew her tea in peace.

Finally, Annie carried her steaming mug into the living room and curled up on the sofa. She pulled a light afghan off the back of the sofa and covered up. She knew she must be sick to need a cover in the summer. Maine summer heat couldn't compare to the summer temperatures back in Texas, but not many Mainers needed a blanket in the middle of the day.

Annie spread the cover over her legs and sipped her tea. She hoped she'd just caught a really short-lived virus. The warmth of the tea soothed her sore throat, and she drew her legs up, curling into the corner of the sofa. She'd just rest her eyes for a few minutes, and then she'd go find a book or her crochet project bag. A quiet afternoon would be just the thing to shake off the cold.

Annie awoke in a shadowy room with a jump that frightened Boots off the end of the sofa. She blinked. What was she doing sleeping in the living room? She felt awful, as if all of her bones had been rearranged in her sleep and now ached. Then the sound of pounding at the front door sunk into her foggy brain. Someone was on the front porch.

She struggled to her feet and ran her hand over her sleep-mussed hair. A glance down at her badly rumpled dress made her groan. She should have changed when she came home from church. She shuffled to the door, amazed at how heavy the front door felt as she dragged it open. Her best friend, Alice MacFarlane, stood outside on the porch, her face creased with concern. "Annie, are you OK? I've been knocking forever."

"I fell asleep on the sofa," Annie croaked.

Alice wrinkled her nose. "You sound awful."

"I feel worse," Annie said. "Do you want to come in? I don't want you to catch my cold."

"I don't catch colds," Alice said. "I have the immune system of a Viking."

"Brave talk." Annie stepped back, letting Alice through. "Do you want me to get you some coffee or something?"

"Why don't I get us both some tea?" Alice said as she began herding Annie back toward the living room. "I know where everything is. You should go sit down."

Annie nodded, not having the energy to argue about her duties as hostess. She shuffled back to the sofa and sank gratefully into the soft upholstery. She spied her teacup on the table beside the sofa and peered inside. It was empty except for some stray cat hairs. Annie suspected Boots had gone after the sweet milky tea after Annie fell asleep.

Alice came into the living room with a tray. She looked at Annie sitting very straight on the sofa and said, "Why don't you go change into something more comfy, and then you can curl up while I talk. I have something I want to tell you, but if I make you sit up, looking so sick, the guilt will kill me."

Annie nodded and headed upstairs to her room to change. Once she was out of the badly wrinkled linen dress, she actually felt less sick. She pulled on some whisper-soft jersey pants in the same cool gray as Boots's fur. *At least now I won't feel grubby from cat fur,* Annie thought as she slipped into a matching cotton sweater.

Once Annie was back on the sofa with a warm mug in her hands and the afghan tucked around her, Alice said, "I got a strange call from Jim."

"Oh?" Annie looked at her friend with interest. She liked Alice's friend, Jim Parker, and it was clear that Jim adored Alice. Even though the rugged photographer did a lot of traveling for his work, he now seemed to spend every moment of his downtime with Alice.

"He finished his last book and has been tossing ideas around with his publisher," Alice said. "Apparently his coffee-table books are selling really well. I guess it's the storyteller in him. His photos tell almost as much of a story as his narrative."

Annie dabbed at her nose with a tissue. "I'm not surprised. I know the photos I've seen were a fascinating combination of eerie and beautiful."

Alice handed her a fresh tissue. "He said he's going in a whole new direction with the new book, and that it was inspired by me."

Annie smiled. She'd heard Jim call Alice his "muse" more than once. "So what's the book going to be about?"

"He wouldn't tell me." Alice stared down into her mug

with a slight frown. When she looked up, her eyes were worried. "He said he's coming to town and has something important to ask me."

"What do you think it is?" Annie asked. "Something about the new book?"

"I don't know, exactly." Annie could tell Alice was wrestling with whatever she intended to say next. Finally it just burst out of her, "I'm afraid he's going to ask me to marry him."

Annie raised her eyebrows. "Well, he *does* love you. Anyone who has seen you two together knows that."

"And I love him too," Alice insisted, "but I like what we have now. Jim's a nomad through and through. We both know that. He'll never settle down, and he shouldn't. It would be wrong for him. But I *like* being settled. I love Stony Point. I love having my own house. I'm a natural nest builder; that's why I do so well selling Divine Décor. I don't want to be a nomad's wife. I don't think I'd be very good at it."

"But you don't know that's what he wants to ask you," Annie said. "Maybe he wants your opinion on his new idea. You know he respects your opinion. Maybe he wants you to travel with him to some local shoot; you've done that before. Maybe he just wants to come and spend time with you and is being mysterious because he knows it piques your interest. Maybe he bought a pet monkey and wants you to help name it. Honestly, with Jim, almost anything is possible."

"True," Alice said, "but that also means it's possible he's coming to ask me to marry him."

"Then you'll have to deal with that," Annie said. "It's worth thinking about, but not panicking over."

"Big talk when it's not you dealing with the question," Alice said. "What if this were Ian we were talking about?"

"What if Ian was asking *you* to marry *him*?" Annie said, blinking in confusion. "I can't see that happening. Have the two of you ever even dated?"

"No." Alice furrowed her brow. "You know, you might be sicker than I thought. I mean how would you feel if you thought Ian was going to ask you to marry him?"

That shocked Annie out of her fever fog. "I don't think I need to worry about that. Yes, Ian and I have become more than friends, but that friendship is core. I don't think he'd want that to change. We're both really happy about the way things are."

"Yes, but you don't really know what could be going on in Ian's head," Alice said.

The conversation was beginning to confuse Annie. She shook her head. "I'm sure Ian likes the way things are."

"And that's what I *think* about Jim," Alice said. "But I realize that I don't really know what might be going on in his head either. What if he asks me, and I say no. Then he just goes away, and I don't have him in my life anymore. How do I live with that?"

"What if he asks you, and you say yes?" Annie said.

"Then what?" Alice leaned back on the sofa and moaned. "Marriage changes everything. You know that. Why would Jim want to change what we have now?"

Annie shrugged slightly. "Maybe he doesn't. You're still only guessing."

"And freaking out," Alice admitted. "I just feel like I need a plan."

"Not everything in life can be planned," Annie said. "Sometimes you just have to go with your instincts in the moment." She reached out and patted her friend's hand. "Jim isn't going to want to lose what you have either."

"You think?" Alice said weakly.

"I know," Annie said. "Try not to worry about this too much."

"OK, right," Alice said. "I need to think about something else. What I really need is a nice rush of Divine Décor and Princessa jewelry parties. They would keep my mind occupied."

"Oh, are things slow?" Annie asked.

"A little," Alice admitted. "Usually tourist season is a boom time, but it's been slower so far. I'm doing fine, but I have to admit, I wish I was crazy busy. Then I wouldn't have time to obsess. Jim wouldn't even say exactly when he's coming here. I don't even know when he might drop the question."

"You do need to think about something else," Annie said, remembering that this was the same Alice who had thought it was time to move on from her jobs just a few months earlier. She pulled the afghan a little higher, wondering again how she could feel so cold in the middle of summer.

Alice looked at her sharply, and then leaned out and touched Annie's forehead. "You're smoking hot. Have you taken anything for this?"

Annie held up her mug. "Tea."

"Do you have any cold medicine?"

Annie frowned. "Cold medicine always makes me so groggy. I never get anything done when I take that stuff. I just end up falling asleep."

"So, you'll sleep. Do you have any?"

Annie nodded. "In the medicine chest in my bathroom upstairs."

Alice hopped up and headed in search of medicine. Annie snuggled deeper into the sofa and thought about Jim. Realistically, he could be thinking about asking Alice to marry him. He certainly loved her. But he was also a bit of an adventurer—a nomad, as Alice had put it—and Annie would be surprised to learn he wanted to change their relationship. It seemed to work well for them.

She leaned her head against the back of the couch. She wouldn't like having that kind of relationship. Alice had to spend so much time away from Jim. And she never really knew when he was going to have time to spend with her. Annie had always liked knowing that Wayne was a total homebody, and she loved that about him. His constancy had been so important to her that she'd found herself looking for him each evening for months after he died. Even now, years after his death, she still expected him to come through the front door from time to time.

She let her mind wander to Ian. Ian would be one of those constant men, someone you could always count on. Even now, he seemed to always be there when she needed him. She pictured his warm smile and the rugged lines of his face. She smiled in return, thinking of how nice it would be if he were there, wrapping her in one of his warm hugs.

She was jerked back to reality when Alice shook her gently. "Here, take this." She handed the cold medicine to

Annie, who swallowed it obediently and then sipped from the glass of water Alice handed her.

A sudden thought struck Annie as she looked at her friend. "The robberies," she said. "You could think about the robberies. A mystery would take your mind off fretting about Jim."

"Right," Alice said as she settled into a chair across from Annie. "I actually know all three of the victims."

"Really?" Annie raised her eyebrows, but was surprised to find they felt heavy. How could eyebrows be heavy? That didn't make any sense. She shook her head lightly to clear it, but that just made her feel dizzy. "Did they have anything in common?"

Alice shook her head. "Well, they all have a lot more money than me, but other than that—not really. Two were summer people, but the latest was someone who lived here year-round. Only one of them went to our church. The first victim doesn't even shop around here. I remember Mrs. Penchant telling me that all the Stony Point stores smell like fish."

"Charming," Annie grumbled.

Alice shrugged. "She bought a lot of Princessa jewelry as Christmas gifts for people in her company, so I can't complain about her. I'll admit I am probably glad not to work for her."

"Were all the victims jewelry clients?" Annie asked.

Alice shook her head. "No, the Dunhams never bought jewelry or Divine Décor from me. I know them just from the church pantry. They both volunteer there sometimes."

"It sounds like the victims didn't have much in common," Annie said.

Alice shook her head, and then paused while she thought for a moment. "Mrs. Penchant has one of those strange hairless cats, and I know Carl Clark has a cat. It's some stray that adopted him. I saw it once. It looked like it had spent some hard years on the street."

"But the Dunhams don't have a cat?" Annie asked.

"No, they have that German shepherd/malamute mix. Do you remember it? Gigantic black and gray thing. I think his name is Bear. They bring it sometimes to community events on the Town Square."

Annie's eyes widened. "I do remember. I often wondered how they manage to feed something that big. Why would anyone break into a house where an animal like that lived? I know he is a nice dog, but even a nice dog doesn't like strangers in his house."

"Well, the dog might not have been there," Alice said. "They might have taken him with them. I can't imagine you would leave something that big at home to destroy your house out of boredom. My mom had a little tiny poodle for years, and the little monster would rip up couch cushions if you left it alone. The Dunhams' dog would probably just eat the whole couch."

Annie felt something nudging her instincts, but she was having trouble concentrating. Finally she said, "But how would the burglar know the dog wasn't in the house? It might have been. Chief Edwards said he was sure the burglar must have cased the homes, so surely the thief knew about the dog. Why not just mark that house off as a possible target?"

"When did you talk to Chief Edwards?" Alice asked.

Annie waved her hand. "I didn't. Peggy was eavesdropping and told Kate."

"Ah, the Stony Point grapevine," Alice said. "We know it well. You know, maybe I could talk to each of the victims and find out what I can. If Chief Edwards thinks the crook was watching their houses, maybe they saw him."

"I could go with you," Annie croaked, her voice raw from so much conversation.

"Maybe," Alice said tentatively. "If you get better. I'm not sure dragging yourself around Stony Point is the best treatment for a summer cold. I'll call you in the morning and see how you feel."

"I'm sure I'll be a lot better," Annie promised. She shivered as a chill passed over her.

"Sure," Alice said. "In the meanwhile, maybe I should fix you some soup. Have you eaten?"

"It's not suppertime yet, is it?" Annie asked. She looked toward the windows and was surprised to find them darkening.

"Yeah, I think you should probably give up on being all better by tomorrow," Alice said, shaking her head. "I'll get you some soup and then leave you to sleep. I promise to call before I set out tomorrow, but I suspect this is one bit of sleuthing that I'll be doing solo for a while."

Annie started to argue, but was caught in a sneezing fit.

Finally she sniffled and said, "Promise you'll fill me in on all the details."

Alice grinned and held up three fingers. "Scout's honor."

~ 3 ~

*I*n the snug carriage house next door to Grey Gables, Alice awoke early on Monday. The sunlight streaming through her bedroom windows reminded her that she'd forgotten to shut the blinds the night before. Her chat with Annie had helped calm her nerves about Jim until she got back to her house and had time to start running Jim's phone call through her head again. He loved surprises almost as much as he liked teasing her, so maybe Annie was right. Maybe she *was* worrying for nothing. For all she knew, he was going to show up at her doorstep looking for names for that monkey Annie had mentioned or some other equally crazy thing.

That brought a smile to Alice's lips. One thing she knew, Jim wouldn't show up with a cat. Annie's Boots had convinced Jim that cats were unpredictable and potentially dangerous. "You never know what a cat might do," Jim had said, his blue eyes sparkling, "just like pretty, red-headed women."

Alice's smile grew. Jim could always make her laugh. Maybe she just needed to trust him. She shook off her worries and walked determinedly to the kitchen for some breakfast and a plan of attack for the day. She seriously doubted that Annie was in any shape to go sleuthing with her, but she'd promised, and she wanted to check on her friend anyway. She wondered if she should just call or walk over.

Alice flipped through her recipes and decided to make a batch of poppy seed muffins for breakfast. She had made muffins so often that her hands almost worked on their own while she thought about her plan for the day. She hoped that throwing herself into the mystery of the break-ins would keep her mind away from troubling relationship worries.

As soon as she poured the batter into the muffin cups, she decided to make something for Annie. She could carry over a couple of muffins for breakfast, but her friend might need more traditional invalid comfort food. She poked around in her fridge and decided to put together a slow cooker of chicken soup. She'd have dinner waiting for her when she got home and have something nourishing to share with Annie. Alice began dragging vegetables out of the fridge, along with a container of chicken left over from a meal earlier in the week.

Alice thought about how much she'd changed since Annie Dawson had moved to Stony Point. She'd known Annie when they were both youngsters. Annie often stayed at Grey Gables during the summer with her grandparents, Charlie and Betsy Holden, since Annie's parents spent so much time overseas on missionary work. As kids, Alice had been the adventurer, the one ready for anything. Annie had been the cautious, stable influence.

Alice knew her own failed marriage had killed much of her adventurous spirit. When Alice came back to Stony Point, she was defeated and ashamed. She'd kept everyone at arm's length—with the exception of Betsy, who had always provided a sympathetic ear—until Annie blew back into her life by moving into Grey Gables after her grandmother passed away. A good marriage and the challenge of raising a child had made Annie a strong, brave woman, while Alice was still reeling a little with the insecurities her ex had drilled into her.

Swinging the fridge door closed, Alice shook her head as she thought about the times she'd been a bit jealous of her best friend. Annie was so comfortable in herself, and men responded to that. Alice had seen the single men in Stony Point sucking in their stomachs as Annie passed by. The amazing thing was that Annie never seemed to notice. She just was what she was. She didn't even color the gray streaks out of her straight blond hair. Annie's cheerful confidence woke Alice up to the things she'd lost in herself.

Though Annie and Alice had bonded over baked goods, needlework, and mysteries, Alice had still felt like the plain sister until she met Jim. To Alice's total shock, Jim had clearly preferred her over her lovely friend. Jim loved Alice's wild auburn curls, forcing Alice to look at them as less of a nuisance and more of a glory all their own. His open admiration of everything about her had helped her get back her own self-confidence. And Alice noticed how the men of Stony Point now sucked in their stomachs as *she* passed by too.

Annie had sparked change in a lot of lives in Stony Point, even lives that were pretty stuck in their ways. She was so relentless in her curiosity. Alice didn't doubt that she and Annie could get to the bottom of the Stony Point break-ins. "Get well soon, my friend," Alice murmured as she chopped up a carrot. "We've got a case to solve."

She hummed to herself as she worked, letting her mind roll over the burglaries. Alice had been to all three homes at one time or another. They were big homes and very well kept. One was very modern, but two were older—a restored Georgian and a big farmhouse. The Georgian had huge shrubberies which would have let the crook hide, but the other houses were in big open yards. As she'd told Annie, she had trouble seeing anything they had in common.

When she'd finally scraped the chopped veggies from her cutting board to her soup pot, Alice grabbed a cup of coffee and her cellphone to start her day of sleuthing. She called Patty Dunham, who picked up the phone on the second ring.

"Hi, this is Alice MacFarland," Alice said. "I hope I'm not calling too early."

"Oh no," Patty said. "I've already been out for a drag with our dog, Bear."

"A drag?"

Patty laughed. "When I walk Bear, I'm just the weight that slows him down a little. I'm so glad you called. I was going to call you."

Alice's eyes widened in surprise. "You were?"

"Well, you know about our break-in?"

"Yes, Reverend Wallace mentioned it on Sunday."

"Oh, right—I was in the nursery with Kate's daughter, Vanessa, helping with the babies. Anyway, one of the things we lost was a huge painting that hung in the living room. Chief Edwards has tried to be upbeat about the chances of our getting back the things that were stolen, but I don't think he *really* expects to find it. So I thought I might buy some nice things to go in that spot … at least until we get our painting back. Connie from church mentioned having gotten some pretty pieces from Divine Décor."

"Oh, yes," Alice said. "Would you like me to bring over a catalog?"

"If you don't mind," Patty said, "and maybe look at the spot. Connie said you have a good eye. Seeing that big bare spot just rubs my nose in the burglary over and over. That's really not good for me."

"I'll be glad to bring it over," Alice said. "When can I drop by?"

"Well, Rob is sleeping in so maybe around eleven," Patty suggested. "Does that work for you?"

"I'll be there." Alice hung up the phone and grinned. That certainly was easy. She looked back down at the phone in her hand. Should she call Annie or let her sleep? Finally she decided to walk over with the muffins and take a look at her friend. Then she'd know for sure.

As on Sunday, Alice had a long wait after she knocked on Annie's door. Finally the door opened. Annie's normally silky hair stuck up strangely on one side of her head. Her nose looked red and raw. Still, she smiled at Alice. "Sorry," she said, her voice husky. "I lost track of time. Come in. I'll run a brush through my hair and get dressed."

"Are you sure you should be going anywhere with your cold?" Alice asked.

"I'm feeling much better," Annie said as she backed away from the door.

Alice looked at her skeptically. "Well, I called Patty Dunham, and she invited me over. She wants to buy some Divine Décor items to fill a void on her wall—a space created when the burglar stole a painting."

Annie stopped her shuffling walk and looked at Alice with interest. "I would think paintings were a specialized market. I mean, everyone knows places where you could sell a television or a computer, but a painting?"

Alice nodded. "I hadn't thought of that. Maybe we should find out what the crook stole from each home."

"I think we should. We'll go right after I change." Suddenly Annie stopped her shuffle and began sneezing again. The string of sneezes was answered by an annoyed yowl from Boots who stood in the doorway to the living room, her fur puffed out.

"Boots hates my cold," Annie said when the sneezes finally stopped. Her "my cold" came out "by code" in her stopped-up state.

"Apparently," Alice said. "You know, I'm not sure how much people are going to open up to questions if you're going to sneeze all over them."

Annie frowned at her. "I'm all done sneezing." As soon as she'd said the words, another string of sneezes started, bringing on more complaints from Boots.

"Honestly, I think you should stay home and get better—or is that 'bedder'?" Alice teased. Then she held up the small covered basket in her hands. "I'll leave you some muffins for breakfast. I'll come by this afternoon and tell you everything I learn. I promise. And I'll bring you some chicken soup for supper—the real stuff, not from a can."

Annie still frowned, but nodded as Alice hustled her into the living room and settled her on the sofa with the afghan and a box of tissues. "Do you want me to get you some tea to go with these muffins?" Alice asked.

"If you don't mind," Annie said meekly.

Once Alice had Annie settled with a cup of tea, some cold capsules, and a warm muffin, she headed over to the Dunhams' house. With the top down on her beloved Mustang convertible, the warm breeze whipped her hair into a wild tangle in spite of her scarf. She ran a hand through her curls but then decided it didn't matter. The day was beautiful. The sun was warm. And her life was nearly perfect.

The Dunhams' home was a beautiful old farmhouse with a tin roof and a wide, welcoming front porch. Driving up the gravel driveway, Alice spotted a beautiful pair of chestnut horses standing in a fenced field. One stomped a front hoof and tossed its mane as Alice passed. The two horses looked identical except for the star on the forehead of the one that totally ignored her passing. As she got out of her car in front of the house, the front door opened, and Bear exploded past Patty Dunham in the doorway. Alice froze in anticipation of the big dog that hurtled toward her. Bear skidded to a halt just in front of her and sniffed her hand politely.

"Sorry about that," Patty called as she walked down the steps. "For a big dog, he can be sneaky. I thought he was asleep in the kitchen."

"That's OK," Alice said. "You know, I'm amazed anyone would dare break in to this place with Bear here."

"I doubt they would have." Patty snapped a leash to the dog's collar. "Bear's a sweetie, but he wouldn't want strangers in the house when we're not here."

"So you had him with you?"

Patty shook her head. "No, he was over in the Stony Point Kennel. Bear's so big they have to keep him in a room all by himself at night. Their metal kennels are just too small. He doesn't mind though. He's always excited to see Margaret."

"Margaret?"

Patty nodded. "Margaret Freeman. She and her husband own the kennel. She just loves Bear and spoils him terribly."

Patty tugged slightly on the leash, but Bear just sat down beside Alice and began leaning heavily on her leg. She took the hint and rubbed his velvety ears while he panted cheerfully and leaned a little harder. "Be careful," Alice told him. "If you lean any more, I'll fall over."

"Well, if Bear doesn't mind, why don't you come on in?" Patty said. "I'll show you the wall I need to decorate."

As they walked through the house, Alice admired the dark hardwood floors in the house and the beautiful aged-wood wainscoting. "All the wainscoting is made from old barn wood," Patty said. "We had to take down one of the outbuildings, so we used it when we remodeled. Since this is our summer place, it gives it a very different look from the apartment we left behind in the city."

"I'm sure," Alice murmured. She couldn't imagine having such a massive home to keep up. She was always proud when she managed to keep her little place clean and organized.

She could spot the empty wall in the living room right away. An art light hung over the bare expanse. "Oh, that must have been a large painting," Alice said. "What was the subject?"

"It was an antique painting from one of the early New England colonial artists," Patty said. "It was common at the time for limners, really just talented sign painters for the most part, to travel around the countryside and do landscapes for landowners. It was a way to show off your farm or landholdings. This one was of an old farm in the autumn. It was quite enchanting. I fell in love with the idea of having a piece of history that also captured our admiration for the countryside."

"It sounds like a wonderful painting." Alice looked around at the rest of the decorating. "I definitely have some things here in the catalog that would help fill that void and look good with what you already have. It's harder to match a really modern decorating scheme, but I think we have several things you'll like."

"Great!" Patty said. "Let me get you a cup of coffee so we can talk decorating for a while." She led Alice to a huge kitchen that blended very modern appliances with some lovely old farmhouse touches.

"You know, you have a very good eye for decorating," Alice said as she admired the room. They settled at a wonderful old table, and Alice pulled her catalog from her purse so they could spend some time looking over the different options. Eventually Patty settled on a lovely print of a mysterious-looking forest and a few small accent pieces to hang beside it.

"Being robbed must have been so upsetting," Alice said when she finally began putting away her order forms and catalog.

"It was," Patty said. "Honestly, if we didn't have Bear, I would have refused to stay here that first night after we got back. It felt like the burglar was still lurking. You know what I mean?"

"I can imagine," Alice said. "You never noticed any strangers paying special attention to your house before you left?"

Patty shook her head. "No, we don't get many visitors outside of local friends or tradespeople we call in."

"Tradespeople?" Alice said. "Are you still remodeling?"

"No, but with such old buildings, we're always having things worked on," Patty answered. "We've had Peggy's husband out here a dozen times. He's such a fantastic handyman. Reverend Wallace recommended him."

"He is great," Alice agreed. She looked around the kitchen again before spotting a sticker on the back-door window. "You have an alarm system?"

"A lot of good it did," Patty said.

"Oh?"

Patty sighed. "It's not really the alarm company's fault. Rob must have left a window open. He swears he didn't, but I know I didn't, and Rob's so forgetful. Plus, he's the one who loves summer air." Patty smiled. "I like air-conditioned air."

"Where was the window?"

"In the laundry room," Patty said. "Which is a weird place to leave the window open, but Rob must have gone in there looking for something and opened a window. You know how humid laundry rooms get."

Alice nodded. It made sense, but she made a mental note to find out if the other homeowners had mysteriously left open windows. She wrapped up her visit, petted Bear a bit more, and headed out. She decided to drop in on Mrs. Penchant with a jewelry catalog and a few questions.

Mrs. Penchant was as cool and superior as usual, but she was a good customer, and Alice focused on that whenever she felt like wincing at the tall, willowy woman's condescending tone. She certainly had no problem steering the conversation toward the break-in. Mrs. Penchant launched into a tirade about the investigation almost as soon as she greeted Alice at the front door.

"How hard can it be to find my sculpture?" Mrs. Penchant asked as she led Alice toward her white leather sofa. "It was one of a kind. I knew I was taking a risk when I bought a home away from the city, but everyone assured me that I would find it restful." She snorted to show her opinion of that idea. "Now, the fate of my beautiful sculpture is in the hands of Barney Fife."

"Actually, Chief Edwards is extremely competent," Alice said loyally.

Mrs. Penchant looked down her nose at Alice. "I'm sure you think so."

Alice swallowed back a response, waiting a moment until she could speak politely. "So you had an art piece stolen too. How horrible for you. I know the Dunhams lost a painting."

Mrs. Penchant waved her hand. "Yes, I heard. It was

some folk-art thing. There is a huge difference between some rustic dabbling of paint and the sculpture that was stolen from *me*."

"Do you have an alarm system?" Alice asked.

Mrs. Penchant looked down her slender nose. "Of course. The burglar triggered it, but clearly the police here simply don't move very fast. The thief was long gone with my sculpture and jewelry by the time they arrived."

"In order to be in and out so quickly, it sounds like the burglar may have known where the valuable pieces were," Alice said.

"Well, I certainly didn't invite any criminal elements into my home," Mrs. Penchant said. "I'm very careful. I imagine it simply took a while for the police to decide to interrupt their doughnut breaks to come and check on my property."

"So you didn't find any windows open," Alice said.

Mrs. Penchant waved a perfectly manicured hand toward the wide expanse of glass that looked out on her perfectly kept lawn. "The windows don't open. I'm prone to allergies, so I don't need outside air coming in."

Alice left the Princessa jewelry catalog, though Mrs. Penchant wearily said she'd bought all the jewelry for the help that she needed until the winter holidays. Alice simply thanked her and stood to leave.

As Mrs. Penchant led her to the door, she carried the hairless cat that Alice thought was so strange looking. The cat sneezed. "Oh, dear," she said. "I do hope you didn't catch something at the kennel."

Alice looked back, interested. "The Stony Point Kennel?"

"Yes," Mrs. Penchant said. "I don't like to leave

Sebastian here alone when I go into the city for more than a day. Mrs. Freeman assures me they don't let him mix with the other animals there, but I do worry. So far I haven't found squirrel fleas or deer ticks on him after a kennel stay, but I am not entirely certain my darling is really safe there."

Alice murmured something vaguely reassuring and left, happy to be outside. Mrs. Penchant's stark decorating scheme always left Alice feeling a little sensory deprived, and the woman's attitude really tested the limits of Alice's tolerance. She hurried out to the Mustang and flipped open her phone as soon as she hit the seat. She called Carl Clark and caught him in the middle of dealing with insurance forms, so he was eager to complain about the burglary as well.

"Art?" he said. "No, I don't really have art. I lost electronics mostly, and my coin collection. Actually, it was my granddad's collection, though I've added to it now and then."

"I know this is a weird question, but do you still have your cat?"

"Weasel? Yeah, I still have him. I can't picture anyone stealing a one-eyed, one-eared alley cat," Carl said laughing. "Besides, he wasn't at the house anyway. I took him to the kennel. I usually leave him at home, but he was on meds. Margaret Freeman is the only person I know who would willingly cram pills into Weasel. I always feel like I should give the poor woman hazardous-duty pay."

Alice felt like whooping. She thanked Carl quickly and rang off. She had found a link joining all three burglaries. Now she just had to figure out what it meant.

— 4 —

On Tuesday morning, Annie awoke to find Boots curled up next to her. Since the cat had been giving her the serious cold shoulder for all the sneezing, Annie hoped her return was a good sign. She sat up slowly and swung her legs over the side of the bed. She didn't feel dizzy or cold. She took a deep breath and smiled. Her head felt clear. Maybe she was all better.

She dressed quickly and headed for the kitchen with Boots meowing insistently at her feet. "Anyone would think I haven't fed you the whole time I've been sick," Annie half-whispered. She froze and tried to speak in a normal tone, but only a whisper came out and even that felt strained. "Laryngitis?" she whispered. "Super."

Annie hoped a cup of hot coffee would both soothe her throat and kick-start her energy. She felt better, but she was having trouble shaking off her morning lag. Boots wove figure eights around her ankles as she started the coffee. The cat dove face first into the bowl as soon as Annie poured in some kibble. Annie was reminded of a nature documentary she had watched once about a type of shrew that had to eat every few hours or it would starve. "Maybe I should have the vet check to be sure you're really a cat," Annie whispered.

She carried her hot coffee to the table by the living room window. The coffee felt incredibly good going down her raw throat. She had a few hours before the Hook and Needle Club meeting, but she was sure she wouldn't get her voice back that quickly.

Annie pictured Stella's face if Annie showed up sneezing and whispering. Stella took her matriarchal position very seriously, and Annie could almost feel the icy disapproval just thinking about her. Still, she hated missing updates on the mystery.

As she was musing, the telephone rang. "How's the invalid?" Alice's cheerful voice asked.

"Feeling better," Annie said, her voice rasping. "But I've lost my voice."

"I'll say," Alice agreed. "I guess that means you don't need a ride to the meeting."

"No I don't, thanks. No one wants my germs," Annie said. "Though I do feel much better with the exception of my voice. Why didn't you come by yesterday after checking out the robbery victims? I thought you were bringing me soup!"

Alice laughed. "I did. I knocked. I waited. I knocked some more. I probably drove Boots crazy."

"Oh," Annie said. "I must have really been sleeping hard."

"That's OK; you needed it. Look, I'll come by right after the meeting. I promise."

"Are you feeling OK?" Annie asked. "You've been around my germs twice now."

"I'm fine," Alice said. "I have an amazing immune

system. I come from a long line of women who were too feisty to get sick."

"No more word from Jim?" Annie asked.

"No," Alice said with a groan. "And I'm trying not to think about it because it's making me crazy. I thought he would call again. He seemed so eager about the whole question thing."

"I'm sure he will," Annie said. She was beginning to really feel the strain from talking on the phone. "I'll see you when you come by this afternoon."

"I'll be there with soup!" Alice promised.

Annie was glad to hang up the phone. She did feel somewhat better, but her throat hurt. And she really didn't feel like going out. Hanging up the phone, she moved to the sofa with her crochet bag. It felt good to just curl up and crochet.

She found the soft colors of the baby blanket she was making and the smooth movement of the hook soothing. Plus, it felt good to be producing something and not just sleeping. As she worked, she felt a mild ache running through her bones, reminding her that she wasn't really well yet. Still, she knew she was getting better.

The soothing repetition of the crochet grew almost hypnotic as Annie let her mind drift so much that she jumped when the phone rang again, knocking the ball of yarn to the floor. She picked up the phone and held it to her ear with a breathy hello while chasing the ball of yarn.

"Mom?" LeeAnn said into her ear.

"Oh, hi, honey," Annie whispered into the phone.

"Are you all right? Is something going on there?"

Annie finally scooped up the yarn ball and settled on the couch with the phone. "I'm fine. I'm getting over a cold."

"If that's how you sound when you're getting over it, you must have been really sick," LeeAnn said fretfully.

"I felt pretty rotten," Annie admitted, "but I actually feel much better now. My voice just doesn't sound like it."

"Oh, I've had that before," LeeAnn said. "I actually called because John and Joanna went to an acting camp after church yesterday, and they're desperate to tell you about it. Are you up for a twin conversation? I can probably hold them off if you're not."

"No, I'm always happy to talk to my grandbabies."

LeeAnn laughed. "Don't let John hear you call him that. OK, here's the big guy."

Annie heard LeeAnn giving whispered orders not to talk too loud or wear Annie out. Then she heard John, speaking in an odd deep voice. "Greetings Grandmama. I am so terribly sorry to hear that you are ill."

"Grandmama?" Annie echoed.

Her grandson dropped his voice to a whisper. "I'm acting. That's my British accent."

"Oh," Annie said. "It was very impressive."

John's voice climbed back to its normal booming excitement. "You liked it? My teacher said it's good for an actor to be able to do accents. He also said I was very good at projecting. That means you can hear me from a long way off."

"You are excellent at projecting," Annie agreed, holding

the phone a bit away from her ear before the excited boy could deafen her.

"Thanks!" John babbled on for a few minutes about a somewhat confusing mishmash of events from the acting camp. Annie mostly made agreeable and supportive noises. Finally her grandson paused for breath, and Annie heard a brief tussle for the phone.

"It's been so long since we've seen you," Joanna wailed. "I miss you so much."

Annie was startled to hear the child sobbing into the phone. "Oh, sweetheart, I'm sure we'll have a chance to get together soon. Please, don't cry."

Joanna's voice changed in an instant to its usual perky chirp. "I know we will. I was *acting*. I mean, I do miss you. I do. And sometimes it makes me sad, but I wouldn't cry about it. I'm way too old for that. I was totally acting. My sad acting is better on the phone, I think, because I can't cry real tears yet—even when I think about sad things. But I'm still practicing."

"Well," Annie said, "you certainly fooled me. I thought it was very believable."

"John thinks he's the better actor," Joanna said. "But I think it's me because it's much harder to make good sad sounds than to make an accent. Don't you think so?"

"I thought you were both very good."

"I know. You have to say that because you're our grand-mother, and John would get crazy jealous. Still, I'm better."

In the background, Annie heard John shout. "No you're not!" She smiled, thinking that John really *was* excellent at projecting.

Finally, she heard her daughter's voice again. "OK, that's enough." LeeAnn's voice grew calmer as she addressed Annie. "I won't keep you since you're still sick," she said. "But I'll call again soon. We need to coordinate for a visit. Herb is doing really well at keeping his promise of making more family time. I want to tell you all about it. But, for now, you should rest and drink plenty of tea."

"I will," Annie promised. "In fact, I'll go make a new cup as soon as we're done. And all I have scheduled for today is crochet."

"Sounds like a good plan," LeeAnn said. "Get well. I love you, Mom."

"I love you too," Annie said.

She hung up the phone and headed for the kitchen to get a cup of tea. Her throat was hurting from the brief phone conversation. When she got back to the sofa, she found Boots curled up on the half-done baby blanket. "That's not for you," she whispered. Boots opened one eye, and then closed it again. Annie set her mug of tea on the table next to the sofa and lifted Boots off the blanket, gently prying the cat's claws from the yarn.

Boots grumbled the whole time until Annie curled up on the sofa again. The cat put a tentative paw on Annie's leg, and then tried to settle comfortably on Annie's curled-up legs. Finally, she managed to wedge herself between Annie and the back of the couch while half-spread across Annie's lap. "Are you sure you have bones?" Annie asked. Boots didn't bother to look up. She just closed her eyes and purred.

Annie took up her crochet again, picking stray cat hairs from the blanket as she spotted them. The rows of smooth, even stitches grew until Annie could cover her whole lap with the warm little blanket. She pictured a missionary mom wrapping her new baby in the blanket's warmth. Annie loved providing that touch of comfort for families far from home. She knew she would soon have the blanket finished and ready to send to the Missionary Cupboard in her church back in Brookfield, Texas. No matter how many years she lived in Stony Point, a little piece of Annie's heart would always be with that warm, caring Texas congregation.

A knock at the door pulled Annie out of her thoughts. She gathered the blanket and slipped it back in the crochet bag. Then she hurried to let Alice in. Alice was carrying a small bag and a large plastic container. She held up the container. "Are you ready for soup?"

Annie glanced at her watch and her eyes widened. She'd worked completely through lunch, which meant she'd had nothing except coffee and tea. She could almost hear a voice in her head, scolding her. "Skipping meals is no way to feed your immune system," Gram always said.

"Soup would be wonderful," Annie croaked. Her voice was a little louder but still strange in her ears.

"You look better," Alice said as she followed Annie down the hall toward the kitchen. "But you sound awful. How do you feel?"

"Still a little achy, but better. I've been crocheting all day and lost track of time."

"Well, that sounds like a step up from sleeping," Alice said as she opened the container and opened a cupboard to retrieve a pot. "Everyone missed you at the meeting. Peggy was going to bring you soup from the diner after work, but I told her I'd made you some. And Kate said to tell you that she forgives you about the youth bake sale at the farmers market."

Annie's eyes opened wide. "Oh, no, I completely forgot that I'd promised to make something."

"That's OK," Alice said. "I donated a batch of poppy seed muffins that I made last night and forgot to take with me to the meeting. So it all worked out fine. Plus, since I had to go to the farmers market to drop off the muffins, I picked up some homemade cheese for you." She reached into the bag and pulled out a paper-wrapped package of cheese, a fresh-baked loaf of French bread, and some fresh vegetables.

"You take good care of me," Annie said.

"Someone came into A Stitch in Time at the end of the meeting looking for you," Alice said. Annie widened her eyes in curiosity. "Our good mayor, of course. He was very concerned to hear that you're sick."

Annie looked horrified, reaching up to touch her hair. She knew it needed a good wash. "He's not coming over is he?"

"He was, but I think I talked him out of it," Alice said. "I said you were recovering well, but sleeping a lot."

"Thanks," Annie said. She settled down at the kitchen table while Alice sliced the bread and some of the cheese and put it under the broiler to toast. Then she poured the hot soup into bowls with the cheesy toast on the side.

"I have other big news," Alice said. "There was another break-in. It happened Saturday night apparently, but no one knew about it until the owners came back from their trip on Monday."

"That's terrible," Annie said.

"The young couple was at The Cup & Saucer this morning, so Peggy pumped them for information. They have two dachshunds that were in the kennel during the robbery."

"The kennel?" Annie repeated.

"Oh, right, I forgot that I didn't get to talk to you yesterday," Alice said. "Every house that was broken into had a pet, and every pet was in the Stony Point Kennel during the robbery."

"That's quite a coincidence," Annie said as Alice put the bowl of soup in front of her. She breathed in the savory smell, and her stomach growled.

"Sounds like your appetite is waking up," Alice said. "That's good."

Annie sipped the soup. "It's the magic of your cooking." She almost moaned as the warm soup slipped down her throat. After a few spoonfuls, she paused to ask, "What did the Hook and Needle Club think of the clues you discovered?"

"They're wildly excited, of course," Alice said. "Peggy is planning to find out if Chief Edwards has followed up on it. Stella plans to call a few art dealers she knows to see if they might know anything about the art that has been stolen, though she was quick to inform us that she does not know anyone who would be involved in anything illegal. Gwen is making a list of everyone in Stony Point who would be tempting targets for a burglar, and then she's going to call and find out which of the people have pets. I believe she's also going to map out which of those people might be planning an out-of-town trip."

"Gwen does know a lot of people," Annie said. Gwendolyn Palmer's husband was the president of the Stony Point Savings Bank, and the two of them were very involved in the town's social scene.

"She definitely knows the sort of people who would be tempting targets for burglars. Unfortunately, no one at the meeting actually knows the people who own the kennel," Alice said. "I think I might have met Margaret Freeman once, but I'm not sure."

"I'm sure Ian knows them," Annie said. "He sometimes boards Tartan there."

"Maybe Ian should be my detecting partner until you're well again," Alice teased.

"Jim would love that," Annie said with a smile as she thought about the rivalry between the two men. She still wasn't certain if they were actually jealous of one another or just territorial. "So, no one at the meeting knew anything helpful about the kennel or the owners? We can usually count on Peggy or Mary Beth for some bits of information on everyone in Stony Point."

"Well, apparently Margaret Freeman is not into crafts, so Mary Beth didn't know anything," Alice said. "But Peggy did tell us that the talk around town is that Mr. and Mrs. Freeman are fighting. From personal experience I know that fights can lead to divorce, and divorce can be costly. Could it be that one or the other is building up a nest egg, anticipating the possibility of a legal battle?"

"It sounds like we need to meet them in person." Annie suddenly perked up as an idea hit her. "If you can wait until tomorrow, I'm sure I'll be well enough to go with you. And I might want to check out the kennel before I take another trip, to see if I want to leave my darling little Boots there."

Alice laughed at the gushy tone Annie put on. "Your 'darling little Boots' would disown you," she said, "but that would be a great cover. Do you really think you'll be up to it tomorrow? I don't want to cause you a relapse."

Annie nodded. "I'm finally feeling human again. I think I'll be well enough to go with you—if you don't mind waiting until tomorrow. I promise not to overdo."

"No problem. It'll give me the rest of the day to worry about Jim." Alice ran her hand through her curls.

Annie stood and began collecting the dishes from their lunch. She smiled gently at her friend. "Try not to make yourself crazy about it."

Alice huffed. "That's easier said than done." She put up a hand as if to fend off whatever Annie might say next. "I know. I'm making myself crazy. I keep reminding myself that he never emails or calls every day. He *does* work. But I can't believe he threw out this mysterious teaser about a *question* he wanted to ask me, and then ...

nothing. I could give him a good shaking just for keeping me awake over this."

"I thought not hearing from him was good news—giving you breathing room. Have you changed your mind about him popping the question?"

"No!" Alice hopped up and started to pace. Annie nearly laughed as she suddenly remembered a time when Jim paced in exactly the same way when he was frantically worried about Alice during one of their mysteries. "I definitely do not want to deal with a question like that, not until I figure out what I want."

"But?" Annie said.

"But waiting for him to drop the bomb is almost worse than actually hearing it. I have this feeling of impending doom, and it's making me jumpy."

Annie gave her a look. "I think 'impending doom' might be just a little overdramatic."

"Maybe a little," Alice admitted.

"And maybe you should call him," Annie suggested. "Then you'd get this over with and not keep driving yourself crazy about it."

"But then he might ask me to marry him," Alice said. "And I still don't know what to say. He can't ask me before I know what answer I want to give him. No; that would be worse than the waiting."

Annie smiled. "I wish I had an answer for you."

Alice sighed and collapsed back onto the sofa. "You and me both."

"Well, tying yourself in knots might just make it harder to decide what you want. Instead of worrying about the question, maybe you should think about your relationship with Jim. Then the answer might work itself out."

"Maybe," Alice admitted. "At least we have a plan for this mystery. Tomorrow, you and I will storm the kennel."

— 5 —

Wednesday found Annie without any of the aches from the last few days. "But can I talk?" she asked herself. Her voice sounded slightly husky to her ears, but it was no longer a strained whisper.

Boots looked up from where she lay curled up beside Annie's pillow. She stretched and gave Annie a disgruntled mew.

"Oh, did I wake you, your highness?" Annie asked the cat. Boots just blinked at her. "Well, I'll get you some kibble just to make it up to you." Annie slipped her feet into her soft scuffs and headed out the door. Boots snapped awake and darted after her, meowing with urgency.

Annie scooped up the cat and hugged her. "I thought you'd come around."

As she poured kibble into the small ceramic bowl, Boots stuck her face directly in the way, causing bits to fly off onto the floor. With an exasperated huff, Annie squatted down to pick up kibble and drop it through the small gaps around the cat's face. "Anyone would think I never feed you," she scolded.

She spotted a piece of cat food just under the edge of the stove. Rather than duckwalk toward it, Annie stretched her arm as far as she could, tilting precariously. Just then her cellphone rang, making her jump, lose her balance, and tumble forward, nearly landing on Boots. The cat yowled in alarm and raced out of the room, tipping over her food bowl in the process.

With a groan, Annie swept the food up with one hand, dumped it back into the bowl, and stood to grab the phone. "Alice?" she said.

"Not this time," Ian's deep, smooth voice said. "I hope I didn't wake you. I wanted to call before I headed to the office. I heard you were sick yesterday."

"It was just a cold," Annie said. "I'm much better, thank you."

"You still sound a little hoarse," Ian told her.

"It's better than yesterday when I was a squeaky whisper." Annie poured a cup of coffee and carried it, along with the phone, to the table. "I really do feel pretty close to normal."

"Do you have enough soup?" Ian asked. "I could pick some up from the diner today and drive it over."

"No, I still have some homemade soup Alice brought over," Annie said. "But thank you for the offer."

"I hope you're not planning to overdo it today," he said. "You probably shouldn't do any yard work or be out in the wind too much. Don't push just because you're feeling better. Your body needs rest to recover."

"I'll be careful, *Mom*," Annie said, chuckling.

"See? You're still delirious," Ian replied, with a chuckle of his own. "I actually had two reasons for calling. I know we had plans to go to the movies this Friday, but I need to be out of town. I probably won't be back before Sunday. I promise to make it up to you next week."

"That's not a problem," Annie said. She hadn't been overly excited about the action movie Ian wanted to see anyway. Ian seemed to judge the quality of a movie by how many things blew up, while Annie liked a good two-hankie love story. "Do you need me to watch Tartan?"

"No, I knew you wouldn't be up to it this time, so he's going to stay at the kennel," Ian said. "He loves it there. They spoil him outrageously."

"Oh." Annie wondered if she should tell Ian about their very vague concerns about the kennel being tied to the break-ins. Ian wasn't always in favor of Annie's sleuthing, though he seemed to have gotten used to it. Still, since he was already worried about her cold, it might be better not to mention her interest in the case.

"Now you sound disappointed," Ian said, breaking into her thoughts. "I wouldn't put off seeing you, but Todd has a line on a boat."

"A boat?" Annie echoed, still mulling over the kennel issue.

"I've been thinking about buying a boat," Ian said. "I love the water, and this one sounds like a good investment."

"Oh, that sounds like fun," Annie said, sounding a tad insincere even to her own ears. She had enjoyed the times she'd gone out on Todd's boat with Ian, but she'd never had much urge to own one.

"You don't approve," Ian said, his voice disappointed.

"No, it's not that," Annie said. "I love the water too. I'm sorry, Ian. I guess I'm still a little muddle-headed from this cold. I really don't know much about boats."

"I'll teach you," Ian promised. "Assuming I buy it, of

course. I haven't even seen it except in a photo. At any rate, am I forgiven for putting off our movie date?"

Annie assured him she was fine with missing the movie night. "Have a good time on your trip," she said. "I hope the boat is just perfect, and I know it'll be nice for you and Todd to spend some time together." Both Ian and his brother were so busy, she knew they didn't see each other much more than Annie saw her family in Texas.

"We'll probably end up arguing about the boat's features," Ian said. "You know how brothers are."

Annie laughed, even though she didn't really know much about having a sibling. She was an only child and had raised an only child. She'd imagined having a sibling was like having a constant friend and support—though LeeAnn's twins had shown her there was plenty of squabbling as well. "Try to come home still friends," she said.

"Not to worry," Ian said. "The arguments never stick. I'll tell you all about them when I get home."

"I'll look forward to it."

After she hung up the phone, she hoped she had done the right thing in not mentioning her concerns about the kennel. As she stood with her hand on the receiver, she heard a sturdy knock at the front door. Annie shook off her musing and hurried down the hall toward the front door.

"Sorry to just show up," Alice said after Annie let her in. "But the phone was busy when I called. I wanted to come over while breakfast was still warm." She held up a covered basket.

"Oh, goodies," Annie said. "You're spoiling me horribly. What do you have today?"

Alice flipped back the tea towel on the basket. "Bran muffins. I thought we should have something substantial before we tackled the kennel today. How are you feeling?"

"Much better," Annie said. "Almost normal even."

They walked back to the kitchen and settled at the table with muffins and coffee. "You seem pensive," Alice said. "Are you sure you feel OK?"

Annie took a sip from her coffee mug before answering. "I'm fine. I talked to Ian just before you got here, and he's going out of town. I didn't know if I should mention our concerns about the kennel before he left."

"Do you think Ian would take them seriously?" Alice asked. "We don't have a lot to go on at this point."

"Probably not." Annie pulled her muffin apart as she scolded herself for fretting.

After breakfast, they tidied up quickly. "We should probably take my car," Annie said as they headed out the front door. "I'm not sure having the wind in my face is the best way to recover from a cold."

"I already planned ahead." Alice pointed toward the driveway. Her Mustang sparkled in the summer sun as it always did. Alice was meticulous about her car. The top was up, something Annie rarely saw before winter. "No wind on you."

"Wow, I know that's a sacrifice."

"Anything for my best friend."

The drive to the kennel would take only a few minutes, but Annie wasn't going to waste the time. "So, do you feel any more settled about how you'll handle the situation when Jim finally calls?"

Alice shook her head. "You know, I'm not really worried about whether Jim and I are compatible enough to be married. We are. We fit together better than anyone I've ever known. I'm not even sure it's the whole thing of his work versus mine. I really do believe we could make it work. Jim and I are old enough to know how to deal with problems."

"But?"

"I guess I'm afraid of being rootless," Alice said. "I feel like I belong here again. I don't want to feel adrift."

"You know, even though I only spent summers in Stony Point when I was growing up, I felt like my deepest roots were here," Annie said. "To me, this was the place that felt like home. Texas was the place my parents rested between mission trips. So it always felt a little temporary. But Stony Point felt permanent. Gram was such a strong anchor for a child. I thought I would never feel completely rooted anywhere else. But then, when I fell in love and married Wayne, my roots were wherever we were together. We could have moved a million times and I would have felt at home."

Alice sighed. "I just don't know if I'm capable of that kind of connection with someone. I certainly never had anything remotely like that with John."

"Well, that's the thing about marriage," Annie said. "You always find out things about yourself that you never expected. I definitely wouldn't judge how well married life will work with Jim on how poorly it went with John. Jim is committed to you. I can tell. John MacFarlane was committed only to himself."

Alice's face grew serious as she thought about the dark years with her ex. "That's the truth," she agreed.

"I still say you could be worrying about marriage when it's the furthest thing from Jim's mind. Maybe he just found some creepy artifact to give you as a gift—knowing Jim, he'd find that pretty exciting and want to ask you all kinds of questions about it," Annie said, hoping to lighten the mood. "Or maybe he just wants to take you on a vacation. Since he's always working on one book or another, he might be pretty excited about just going somewhere purely for fun."

Alice nodded, but her face stayed serious the rest of the way to the kennel. They pulled up to the huge circular drive and stopped in front of the building, a New England cape that appeared to have additions by Frankenstein. The original structure had the clean lines Annie saw in many older homes in New England, but from the back a T-shaped addition had been added to house the kennel's boarders.

As soon as Annie got out of the car, she could hear barking. "I can just imagine how Boots would respond to all that barking," she said.

"You'd need to get her cat therapy," Alice agreed cheerfully.

They walked up to the main house where a small sign declared it the "Stony Point Kennel." The main building was clad in cedar siding and painted a soft gray. The burgundy front door stood in sharp contrast against the gray and the clean white trim. Annie opened the door and walked into a spacious room with comfy chairs, a small display of pet merchandise, and a beautiful antique desk used as the reception area.

A young woman sat behind the desk. As soon as she spotted Annie and Alice, she slipped a bookmark into the book she was reading and stood to greet them. "Welcome to Stony Point Kennel. May I help you?"

Annie and Alice introduced themselves. "I have a cat named Boots," Annie said. "She's never been in a kennel, but I'm considering a short trip, and all my friends are so busy this time of year. I thought I might bring her here, but I'm a little nervous about it. Boots is so persnickety."

Annie heard Alice murmur, "That's for sure."

"Ah, well, we have calmed many persnickety pets around here. Let me show you around. I think you'll be pleasantly impressed." The young woman offered her hand. "I'm Marcie Freeman."

"Oh, I heard the owners were named Freeman," Annie said. "But I expected someone older."

"My aunt and uncle own the kennel," the girl said. "I help out here in the summer."

Annie let her eyes drift to the desk and Marcie's book: *Veterinary Anatomy.* "You're studying to be a vet?"

Marcie smiled brightly. "I'm in my third year. My aunt and uncle think having a vet on premises would be a huge help to the business." She led them from the large room, walking by a steep stairway. Annie noticed the stairs were roped off to keep people from wandering upstairs.

Marcie caught Annie's gaze and said, "My aunt and uncle live upstairs. That means there is always someone on premises. Our clients are never alone."

"Oh, that's convenient," Alice said. "Especially if older pets have special medical needs."

Marcie nodded and continued on until they reached a lovely oak door. She led them into what looked like a vet's treatment room. "My aunt is trained as a vet tech and can handle most small problems right here."

"That's good," Annie said as she drifted around the room. She saw a glass-front cupboard of bandages, disinfectant, and a number of different medicines. "Wow! You have a lot of medicine here."

"Those are all meds the current animal boarders are taking," Marcie said. "They're all tagged with the animal's name and information. You'd be surprised at how many pills we have to administer every day. So if your cat is on any medication, we're very experienced in handling that."

"There's no lock on the cabinet," Annie said. "Don't you worry someone might want to break in and go after the drugs? I know they're pet medications, but I always imagined drug addicts weren't very picky."

Marcie laughed. "I don't know that a lot of drug addicts are looking for medications for cat urinary problems or dog heart conditions. I really don't think they have much street value. And with all of us here needing access to these, it's just easier not to have locks. Besides, can you imagine casing this place during the day and hearing all that barking? I think that would be pretty scary."

"I'm surprised the neighbors don't complain about the barking," Alice said.

Marcie rolled her eyes. "Well, one does. My aunt and uncle had to do some major remodeling to better soundproof the night kennels. Really, you cannot hear the barking after we close all the windows in the room where the dogs stay every night. You'll know what I mean when you see the setup."

She led Annie and Alice out of the medical room and into a back lounge with a small kitchen area. A long-legged teenage boy with a mop of dark hair sat at a worn wooden table, eating a sandwich.

"This is Jensen Lees," Marcie said. "He's a huge help around here. And this is Mrs. Dawson and her friend Mrs. MacFarlane. Mrs. Dawson is considering boarding her cat."

The boy nodded and held a hand in front of his mouth as he mumbled a garbled greeting. Marcie gave him a disapproving look, but the boy just shrugged.

"I'm sorry to interrupt your lunch," Annie said.

"Having a little kitchen is nice," Alice said.

Marcie laughed. "Yes, though you really never know what you might find in the fridge. Sometimes Aunt Margaret stores pet meds in there, and once I found a plastic carton of some kind of horrifying worms."

"We were boarding a bird," Jensen said. "The mealworms were part of his diet. You should see what goes in there when we board Jake Myer's snake."

"A snake!" Alice looked around the room in alarm.

"No snakes here right now," Marcie assured her.

The group turned as the back door opened, and a tall woman with white hair walked in. She wore jeans and a flannel shirt, and was wiping her hands on a rag. "Oh, I see we have guests."

"Aunt Margaret, this is Annie Dawson and Alice MacFarlane," Marcie said. "Mrs. Dawson is considering boarding her cat with us."

"Annie Dawson," Margaret said, clearly recognizing the name. "You're Betsy Holden's granddaughter, aren't you? I liked your grandmother a lot. I even met your grandfather once. He was already retired from his veterinary practice by then, of course, but he was a fountain of knowledge about animals."

"My grandparents were the wisest people I've ever known," Annie said. "Did Gram ever board Boots here?"

"Oh no," Margaret said. "She used to tell me that she doubted the kennel would survive. Is that the cat you're considering boarding with us?"

"Yes, though I'm not sure," Annie said. "Boots really doesn't like dogs. Hearing them would drive her wild."

"Ah, well, you should come and see our cat wing." She turned to her niece. "I'll take over with Annie and Alice now. You can go back to the front desk in case anyone comes to pick up a pet." Marcie nodded and gave Annie and Alice a cheerful finger wave before heading back toward the front.

Margaret led them through a door Annie had assumed would go to a mudroom. Instead it led into a short branching hallway. Margaret turned left and led Annie and Alice into a large, clean room. The white walls were lined with rows of cat kennels. Each row had an upper and lower kennel. The kennels themselves were large with smooth walls and floors. Each cat had a fuzzy wall shelf to perch on and a litter box at the bottom.

In the middle of the room, a huge carpet-covered kitty playground took up much of the room. "Each kennel is completely cleaned daily. Those fuzzy coverings on the perching shelf are removable, and each is run through the wash every day. During the cleaning, the cat gets some playtime out here. We are very serious about having a clean facility because it's so easy for animals to pass along ill-nesses if we aren't."

"This room is so quiet," Alice said. "I can't hear the dogs at all."

"Special soundproofing," Margaret said. "We don't want to stress our more sensitive guests. So Boots wouldn't be hearing dogs during the day or the night. And we have an-other small room for guests who need to be kept separate even from the other cats."

"I think Boots would be fine with other cats," Annie said tentatively. "You know, just for my own curiosity, may I see the dog areas? I know Ian Butler keeps Tartan here some-times when he's out of town, and I've often wondered what it was like."

"Oh, you know Ian?" Margaret said. "Tartan is one of our favorite guests. He's such a charmer."

"He is that," Annie agreed. *Tartan is a lot like Ian that way*, she thought.

Margaret led them back down the hallway, taking the other branch. She led them into a huge room, more than twice the size of the cats' accommodations; the clean white walls were lined with dog kennels, and tall windows let in a pleasant breeze. Most of the kennels were empty, but at least a half-dozen dogs jumped to their feet as the women came in. Annie smiled at the line of wagging tails and eager faces.

"They seem happy," Annie said.

"They think it's their turn to go outside. We take the dogs out in shifts since we have fewer outdoor runs than indoor kennels," the thin woman said. Then turning her at-tention to the dogs, she added, "Soon; you'll go out soon."

At the word "out" the tails wagged even more furiously.

"This room is very clean," Alice noted, looking around.

"We clean every kennel every day," Margaret said as she walked over and stroked the ears of a cocker spaniel through the cage bars. "Jensen does most of the kennel cleaning and dog walking. The dogs are crazy about him."

"He seems like a nice young man," Annie said.

"He is. Though I think he's more comfortable with dogs than with people."

"He looks so young," Annie said. "Does he just work in the summer?"

"No, he's here year-round. He quit school a little early, but my husband is helping him study for the GED. Jensen had a tough time when he was younger, but I've never had any reason to complain about his work. He's really a tremendous asset around here."

Alice gave Annie a meaningful look. At least one person at the kennel seemed to have a past. Still, Annie didn't think they should jump to conclusions. They followed the kennel owner to a far door and were soon outside. All across the backyard were pens with large sturdy sheds at the ends.

In each pen, a dog raced to the bit of fence closest to the women and barked. "Wow, they can be loud when they get going," Annie said.

"You can see why they all come inside at night," Margaret said. "Obviously no one wants to hear that all night."

"And some people don't even like to hear it during the day."

The women turned to face a stocky, white-haired man

who walked toward them. "Ah, here's my husband now," Margaret said. "Maynard, this is Annie Dawson and Alice MacFarlane. Annie is Betsy Holden's granddaughter."

"So you've had complaints about the barking from neighbors?" Annie asked.

"One neighbor," Maynard said, nodding toward the back corner of the property where thick shrubbery partially hid a house. "We did a huge remodel to increase our soundproofing, but Bryan Norman still complains. He just switched from noise to smell as his topic."

"Not so much lately," Margaret said consolingly. "He hasn't stormed over with a list of complaints in nearly two weeks." Then she frowned slightly. "Though the smell complaints were totally unfair. We've *never* run a smelly kennel."

"So, do you have any idea why he hasn't complained much lately?" Alice asked.

Maynard shrugged. "Who knows? Maybe he just got tired of being so unpleasant. I just hope he doesn't start back up again. The missus and I were just about fed up with it. Honestly, sometimes I wonder if it wouldn't be better to just get out of the business."

"That is something we never really considered," Margaret said sharply. "Bryan Norman is not running us out of a business we put so much into. Besides, as I said, he seems to have stopped complaining."

Maynard harrumphed. "He's probably just thinking up some new complaint—like fleas."

Margaret looked shocked. "Our clients do *not* have fleas."

Maynard shrugged again. "They don't smell either, but that didn't slow Norman down."

Annie felt guilty about stirring up what was clearly a touchy subject between the husband and wife. "This is certainly a lovely kennel," she said. "I can see why Ian is comfortable leaving Tartan here."

"Tartan?" Maynard's face brightened. "Now there's a one. It's impossible to stay blue around that dog."

"I've often thought that myself," Annie admitted.

Margaret began shepherding them back toward the outer door. Alice paused, looking down at the door curiously. "You have some odd scratch marks around your locks," she said.

"They've been picked," Margaret said. "We managed to lock ourselves outside last Thanksgiving. Luckily we had Jensen. He picked the lock for us. I was never so glad for an employee's misspent youth in my life." The thin woman laughed merrily at the memory.

They filed into the building and back to the main part of the house. They'd barely come through the door when Marcie met them, her expression strained. "Isabelle Murkleson is here."

Margaret groaned softly; then she forced her expression into more cheerful lines and walked toward the front desk. An over-dressed young woman with teased blond hair stood impatiently, clutching her purse. The head of a tiny Pomeranian peeked over the edge of the purse and yapped at them as they approached.

"I have an unexpected trip and need to board Paris," the young woman said. She scooped the dog from the purse and thrust it at Margaret. "I was certainly not going to hand my little darling over to the hired help. You know how delicate his nerves are."

"My niece would have taken good care of Paris," Margaret assured her, but the woman simply sniffed. "I'm surprised to see you so soon, Miss Murkleson. You've barely been home a day since your last trip."

"In my line of work, I never know when I'll be called away. I'll be back for Paris on Monday." The woman promptly turned on her spike heels and marched out of the building.

Margaret sighed and handed the dog to her niece.

"Poor little guy," Marcie said. "I don't know why people have dogs if they aren't going to spend any time with them."

As Marcie carried the little dog out of the room, Annie suddenly sneezed. The first sneeze led to a chain of rapid-fire sneezes.

"Oh my," Margaret said. "I hope you're not allergic to dogs."

Annie shook her head. "I'm getting over a cold. We should be going. Thank you so much for showing me the facility here. It's quite impressive."

"We'll look forward to hearing from you if you have a kenneling need for Boots," Margaret said as they left.

As they walked toward the car, Annie caught Alice's arm. "I think it would be worthwhile to snap some photos of the picked lock," she said. "We should take a quick walk to the back of the building."

"Sounds good."

The two women skirted the building quickly. They spotted Maynard rolling up a hose and quickly hid behind the corner of the house. Thankfully he went through the back door and into the kennel.

They hurried across the back lawn. Alice snapped the photos, and they turned to leave just as they heard the doorknob turn. Alice and Annie exchanged a panicky glance and then ran for the side of the house. At the corner, they peeked around to see Jensen walking out with a handful of leashes. He didn't even glance in their direction, so they sighed in relief and headed for the car.

When they were finally out on the road in the Mustang, Alice asked, "Do you think we should email the photos to Chief Edwards?"

"I don't want to tell him what to do," Annie said. "And we'd probably get a lecture on being involved with an actual police investigation."

"Still, he might find it interesting that the kennel employs someone who knows how to pick locks."

Annie nodded. "Jensen Lees would also know when their clients were going to be out of town."

"Do you think we're on the right track?" Alice asked.

"I don't know, but it's certainly suspicious." Then Annie smiled a little. "Though, it does seem a little too easy. When are our mysteries ever this easy?"

"True," Alice said with a laugh. "We haven't even gotten any mysterious phone calls or notes. What's a mystery where neither of us is threatened or kidnapped?"

"An improvement," Annie said wryly. "A big improvement."

When Annie got home, she listened to her answering machine and discovered a call from LeeAnn. "Hi, Mom. Since you're not answering the phone, I assume you're all better and out running around. Still, if you have a second, please call, just so I don't spend any time imagining you've passed out in your room with a fever with Boots sitting on your chest demanding supper."

Annie laughed at the image as she settled on the couch to call LeeAnn. Her daughter had captured exactly what Boots would do. The cat definitely found Annie's illness an annoying inconvenience.

The phone rang a few times and LeeAnn's voice mail picked up. "I got your message. I was out with Alice," Annie said. "I'm feeling much better and plan to get to bed early. No collapsing, fever, or cat attacks. I love y'all."

She smiled fondly as she hung up the phone and stretched. She felt a bit achy after being out all day. It was definitely time for some hot soup and her jammies. Life's mysteries could wait another day.

— 6 —

Thursday began with Alice in an organizing mood. Since she and Annie hadn't been able to come up with any other leads on the break-ins, she decided to spend the day going through her customer records. She especially needed to make a plan for the people who hadn't bought anything in a while. Did they need a follow-up call? Did any of the new products seem like a good fit with what they'd bought in the past? That kind of work was time-consuming and more than a little subjective, but Alice had been able to revive several lagging client relationships after such organizational days in the past.

She spread out the customer files and all her product pamphlets on her dining table and settled down with a tall mug of coffee. Three coffees and one caffeine-induced case of nerves later, she'd gone through most of the files and all of her first pot of coffee. She was feeling a strange combination of accomplishment and tension.

The knock at the front door made her jump. *OK, time to switch to herbal tea*, she thought as she got up. Walking to the door, Alice wondered if maybe Annie had had a brainstorm about the mystery and was eager to share it. The thought made her smile. She'd enjoy that diversion.

"Hi, gorgeous!" called a familiar voice as she swung the door open.

Alice's smile widened. "Jim!"

"Miss me?" he asked, his deep gravelly voice turning the words into a film noir moment.

"Miss you?" Alice threw her arms around Jim's neck, smothering him with kisses. He put one arm around her; the other held the cane he used to keep his balance on his artificial legs. Jim had lost both legs years earlier in an explosion when he was working as a war photojournalist.

Finally, Alice led him into the house. "You should have told me you were coming," she scolded. "I would have cleaned up a little."

"Then how would I know all your secrets?" Jim teased. He looked around Alice's tidy house. "Besides, if this is how the house looks when you need to clean up, you must hate seeing how I live."

"You mean the way your suitcases just seem to belch clothes all over whatever room you're staying in?" Alice asked. "It doesn't scare me much."

"What's impressive is that you didn't rush around cleaning it up," Jim said as he limped along behind her. "Clean freaks normally spend a lot of time trying to convert others to their evil tidy ways."

"Maybe I'm just keeping my evilness in check." She led him into the dining room and swept her arm in a theatrical gesture toward the table covered with papers. "See, I'm not always neat."

Jim laughed. "You can't fool me, Red. I know that every one of those little piles has an exact purpose."

"Maybe," she said. "Would you like some coffee? I'll have to make another pot; I drank the first one."

"I'll pass, and unless you've been up since the middle of the night, you probably don't need any more. But I wouldn't say no to a glass of milk and whatever you've baked recently."

"Bran muffins," Alice said as they walked on to the kitchen. "I have a few left over from my breakfast with Annie yesterday before we went sleuthing."

Jim opened her fridge and pulled out the jug of milk. "That's my girl. What new mystery is on?"

"Break-ins all over Stony Point," Alice said as she took a plastic container of muffins out of the cupboard and opened it. The smell of brown sugar and spice filled the kitchen. "All the victims had pets in the local kennel. We visited the kennel and found out the young man working there can pick locks."

Jim shrugged. "So can I. Doesn't prove anything."

Alice looked at him with raised eyebrows. "You can? I learn something new every day."

"You know it." Jim's eyes twinkled as he turned his crooked smile toward her. Then he sipped from his mug of milk. "Any other reason to suspect the lock-picking youth?"

"Not really," Alice admitted. "Though the kennel owner did say the young man had been in some trouble in the past."

"Haven't we all?"

"So you're saying we shouldn't jump to conclusions."

Jim shrugged. "I am not about to tell two strong-willed, beautiful women what to do. Now, aren't you going to ask me why I'm here?"

Alice shifted nervously. "Something about a question?"

"First, news." Jim took another long sip from his mug to

stretch out the tension, his blue eyes dancing as he watched Alice frown impatiently. "I had a chat with my publisher. My books have been doing well—really well. They want to go bigger and sexier."

Alice laughed. "Sexier than abandoned theme parks and haunted lighthouses? I can't imagine."

Now it was Jim's turn to laugh. "The new book will be called *Cities of Love*. It's going to be a photographic tour of the most romantic cities in the world."

"Oh, that sounds amazing," Alice said. "What cities are you planning to feature?"

"New York, Paris, Venice," Jim said. "The list is long."

"Sounds like that is going to be a big project."

He nodded. "I'll be living out of a suitcase for a year at least. You know, I can't imagine trying to portray these beautiful, romantic places without my best girl right there. I'm hoping you'll come with me."

"That's the question?" Alice asked. "Will I go with you?"

"That's the one."

She blinked, trying to process the one question she and Annie hadn't imagined. Jim waited patiently while she postponed answering, hopping up and fiddling with getting them more napkins.

"A year of living out of a suitcase?" Alice said, finally. "Standing around, holding your cameras for you? I don't know. I've had a lot of fun when I've gone on short projects with you. And you know I love your company. But a year? I'm going to have to think about that."

Jim nodded, though he looked disappointed. "You know I'm going to do everything I can to sway your decision. With you along, it'll be a fantastic project. Without you, it'll just be lonely."

Alice smiled. "I'd be hurt if you didn't try to convince me to come along." She watched Jim shift in his seat, looking for the most comfortable position. So this was the question she'd worried about so much. Alice was relieved. At least that's what she told herself as she pushed down the small twinge of disappointment. Taking off on a yearlong trip was ridiculous enough. There's no way she could manage that, but at least it wasn't a proposal. She sighed softly. Maybe what the rest of the Hook and Needle Club said about Jim was true—he just wasn't the marrying kind. What a relief.

So why didn't that make her as happy as she expected?

"Penny for your thoughts, Red," Jim said.

"Just thinking about how much I missed you."

"Then why do you look so sad?"

Alice didn't know what to answer to that one. She leaned forward and put her hand over Jim's rough knuckles. "I'm not sad. My face just looks like that when I'm thinking."

"Sure." Jim put his other hand over Alice's. "Far be it from me to argue with a lady."

*   *   *   *

Annie was running the sweeper over her floors at Grey Gables and scolding herself for letting her house get so dusty while she was sick. She felt much better with only the slightest sore throat and a dusty house to remind her of the last few days.

Boots soon made it very clear that she did not

consider vacuuming to be an improvement over sneezing. She flounced off to Annie's bedroom and spent the morning sulking on Annie's bed.

When Annie finally felt the house was clean of all germs and dust, she made a tomato sandwich with one of the ugly but delicious heirloom tomatoes Alice had brought her from the farmers market. She sat down in front at the kitchen table to go through her crochet pattern books. Since she'd finished the baby blanket, she felt like trying something new.

She picked a gorgeous little blanket done is small squares— some of the squares were simple granny squares, but others were filet crochet with adorable animals on them. The granny squares would give her a chance to use up all the short ends of baby yarn, but she'd need a run to A Stitch in Time to get the yarn for the filet crochet squares. She jotted down a note about the recommended yarn in the little notebook she always carried in her purse. Just as she slipped the notebook back in the purse, she heard a knock at the front door.

She hurried down the hall, bursting into a grin at the sight of Jim and Alice on the front porch. "Hi!" she said, throwing open the screen door. "What a surprise. I didn't know you were coming to town."

"You know how much I like surprises," Jim said.

"And you're always so full of them," Alice teased.

Annie led them into the living room. They settled down on the sofa and Annie sat nearby. "So, how's the cold?" Alice asked.

"Well, I cleaned house all morning and didn't sneeze once," Annie said, "which is pretty impressive with all the dust on everything."

"Ah, if that's not proof of healing, I don't know what is," Alice said.

"Sounds like proof of insanity to me," Jim said, shaking his shaggy head. "You both live in houses that look like showroom models."

"You didn't see it yesterday when my primary decor was used tissues," Annie said. "Plus, I couldn't stand the dust anymore."

"I like dust. It makes furniture look like antiques." Jim grinned wickedly as both women made disgusted faces. "So, Alice tells me you two are dabbling in a new mystery."

"Barely," Annie said. "She told you about the break-ins?"

Jim nodded. "And about the kid who knows how to pick locks."

"Jim is skeptical about Jenson's guilt," Alice said, "if you couldn't tell by his snarky tone. He relates to a kid who gets into trouble and picks locks. I think he's nostalgic for his own misspent youth."

"Hey, too much good behavior is boring," Jim said. "And who says it's all relegated to my youth?"

"Well, we don't have a long string of suspects at this point," Annie said. "It could be completely coincidental that all the victims had pets in the kennel."

"Sounds like kind of a big coincidence," Jim said. "Judging from the incidents in the past, how soon do you expect the guy to break into another house?"

"He's been busy," Alice answered. "There have been a couple break-ins a week, and the kennel was full of potential victims when we visited."

"So it might be good if you two could find which of

the patrons with pets in the kennel right now are wealthy enough to be enticing to the burglar," Jim said.

"Well, we know about the woman with the purse dog," Alice said. "Did you take a look at that purse? That purse cost more than my whole wardrobe, or I'll turn in my fashion-spotter decoder ring."

"Did you get the woman's name?" Jim asked.

"Murkleson," Alice responded. "Isabelle Murkleson."

"Wow," Annie said. "I would not have been able to call up that name so fast. I wasn't even sure we heard her first name."

"It's a gift," Alice said loftily; then she shrugged. "Plus, I have to learn names fast. It helps in my sales." She pulled her phone out of the pocket of her cotton cardigan. "Now to put the Hook and Needle Club sleuths to work."

Annie smiled as Alice rang up Gwen to ask if she knew anyone named Isabelle Murkleson, and if she could provide an address. To no one's surprise, Gwen could. She and her husband, John, the president of Stony Point Savings Bank, ran socially with all of the town's upper crust. Their friend could be a bit of a social elitist at times, even though she'd never looked down her patrician nose at either of them.

"Got the address," Alice said with a grin. "Anyone up for a stakeout?"

"I'm in," Jim said. "As long as you ladies wrap up the mystery by the time I have to leave for the first photo shoot in New York City. I'm planning to take one of you with me, and I hate to break up the mystery duo."

"Now, Jim, you know Ian would never let you haul Annie to New York."

"What a disappointment," Jim teased back.

"You're starting a new book?" Annie asked.

"On romantic cities around the world," Jim said. "I'm starting close by so I can show Red how much fun we'll have if she runs away with me to Europe."

"Sounds exciting," Annie said.

"It could be," Jim agreed. "Though it could also be lonely if I have to go all by myself." He turned sad eyes toward Alice.

"I am not moved by the puppy eyes," Alice said.

"I'm too old to be a puppy. I was going for hound dog," Jim said. He turned to Annie. "And speaking of old dogs, how's your mayor friend doing?"

"He's fine," Annie answered. "And he's not old. He went to Rhode Island with his brother to look at a boat."

"They don't have enough boats around here to look at?" Jim said.

"Ian's thinking of buying one."

"He's getting into lobster fishing? I thought the Butlers were into lumber. Don't they own the local sawmill?"

Annie nodded. "I think Ian leaves the lobster fishing to his brother. I believe he has more leisure plans for the boat, if he buys it. Ian loves the water. Though I do believe he intends to rent it out when he's not using it."

"But not for lobster fishing?" Alice added.

"Not hardly. It's not a fishing boat."

"Sounds like your friend may be having a classic midlife crisis," Jim said. "I've seen his flashy car. Now he's buying a boat. The next thing you know, it'll be a motorcycle. I can just picture you perched on the back of his bike, both of you in black leather."

Annie and Alice burst into laughter. It wasn't that Annie would mind seeing Ian in a leather jacket and motorcycle chaps, but it simply wasn't conceivable. She always found it a little startling when she saw him in jeans on weekends.

"I think Ian is probably the least likely man I've ever met to have a midlife crisis," Annie said.

"I don't know," Jim said. "It's those repressed types you have to watch."

"Well, I appreciate your advice," Annie said. "I'll keep an eye out for black leather." Then she and Alice dissolved again into giggles.

7

After an early dinner at the Grand Avenue Fish House, Annie, Alice, and Jim drove farther out on Grand Avenue to the small housing development of oversize, overly modern homes that faced the beach. Isabelle Murkleson's house looked nearly identical to the other four homes, though hers sported a useful high hedge next to the road to help deaden the traffic sounds. Alice parked the Mustang behind the hedge, and they got out of the car.

They crept along behind the hedge as quietly as they could. Annie felt a little silly, slinking around in the night like something from a bad television show. Still, she had to admit, it was more fun than huddling on her sofa sneezing. At the end of the hedge, Annie and Alice peeked around at the driveway.

"There's a car in the drive," Alice whispered.

"Does it belong to the owner?" Jim asked.

Annie shrugged. "I didn't see her car at the kennel. She got there after us and left before us."

"That car certainly looks like the kind she would have though—sleek and expensive," Alice added.

"Well, if the burglary game pays well, I suppose our bad guy could afford a nice car," Jim said.

"It's not exactly unobtrusive," Annie said.

Jim limped to the end of the hedge and peered around.

He turned back and shrugged. "In this neighborhood, that might be unobtrusive."

Alice huffed in frustration. "We're going to have to get closer."

"Well, I should probably stay here." Jim rapped his cane lightly against one leg. "I'm not exactly built for slinking through the darkness. Scream if you need me."

Annie and Alice slipped around the end of the hedge and began walking slowly across the lawn, sticking as close as they could to the strip of landscaping that bordered the driveway. Suddenly, bright lights flashed on all around them, lighting up the night starkly. The women had reached a place where three mature hydrangeas, bursting with flowers, stood in a tight row. The weight of the flowers pulled the branches over and the women dove for the shadows cast by the branches.

They lay still on the ground, barely daring to breath. Annie heard voices from the house ahead of them. The sound came from well above their heads, and Annie remembered the balcony she'd seen when they pulled up.

"It's probably the neighbor's hideous afghan hounds." Annie recognized the haughty voice immediately as Isabelle Murkleson. "They let those dogs run loose to defecate on lawns all over the neighborhood. I've complained over and over. You wouldn't see me letting my precious Paris run around loose."

"I don't see any dogs," a male voice responded. "I don't see anything. Maybe the sensors are malfunctioning."

"Or maybe the dogs ran on to poop on someone else's grass."

Annie risked turning her head slowly for a peek up at the balcony. What she saw made her gasp sharply. She froze again in panic, desperately hoping no one had heard her.

"Did you hear something?" the male voice asked.

"Only my romantic mood draining away," Ms. Murkleson whined. "Come back in. I'm tired of staring at an empty lawn. And talking about dogs is making me miss my little Paris."

"You didn't have to take him to the kennel," the man said. "We could have locked him in a bathroom—or the microwave."

"Martin! I can't believe you said that! You know Paris was just trying to protect me."

"I know I'm a little tired of torn pant legs, ragged socks, and those little needle teeth marks in my ankle," the man answered. "And imagine if he'd gotten up on the bed with us! He could reach something ... well, you know what I mean."

"Oh, Martin, you naughty man!"

Just as the security light switched off, the man laughed. "I was thinking of my nose, but let's go back inside and discuss other options."

Ms. Murkleson and the man walked back into the house. Annie noticed Alice was shaking. "Alice, are you OK?" she whispered.

Alice turned to face Annie and giggled. "That was hysterical."

"You say that because you didn't have to see them standing on the balcony in their birthday suits," Annie said, and then her own small giggle slipped out.

"We better get out of here," Alice said.

The two women crawled backward toward the hedge. By staying low they managed not to trigger the motion-sensor lights again.

When they finally reached the hedge, they found Jim clearly agitated. "Are you OK?" he asked. "I nearly had a heart attack when the lights came on, and I saw you two dive for the ground."

"I'll be feeling that maneuver tomorrow," Alice said, rubbing a sore elbow. "At least we weren't seen. And I think this house is safe from the burglar for the night."

"Apparently Ms. Murkleson's gentleman friend doesn't get along so well with the dog," Annie said. "My guess would be that that's the reason the dog has spent so much time at the kennel lately."

Jim nodded, rubbing a hand over his beard. "So if the burglar did come out to rob the place, he would have found out the same thing you did—that the place wasn't really empty."

"And Ms. Murkleson would probably have made the same assumption if the burglar tripped the lights or made a sound," Alice said. "She would have gone out on the balcony and blamed it on the neighbor's dogs."

"So that stakeout was a bust," Jim said. "We should head home."

"It wasn't a total waste," Alice teased. "Annie got to see a show."

"And I'm going to spend the rest of the night trying to put that totally out of my head," Annie assured her. "If I'm lucky, it won't come back to haunt me in my dreams."

By the time Alice and Jim dropped off Annie, she was

beginning to feel the effects of such a busy day so soon after being ill. She shuffled through changing her clothes and crawled into bed. Boots quickly hopped up on the bed and cuddled up beside Annie for the night. Annie was asleep almost instantly.

Annie's concerns that her experience on Isabelle Murkleson's lawn would visit her dreams turned out to be groundless. Instead, Annie found herself dreaming of Ian's house. She was seated in one of the dark leather chairs in Ian's den, her legs curled up under her for comfort. The room was dimly lit and more shadowy than Annie had ever seen it. Ian was seated at his desk, working with his back to her.

"Maybe you should turn some lights on," Annie said. "It can't be good to work in the dark."

Ian didn't answer, but only bowed his head closer to whatever lay on the desk.

Annie stood and walked toward the desk. Though the chair was only a couple feet from the desk, she walked and walked without getting any closer. "What are you working on?"

Ian didn't answer, keeping his head hunched over his work. Annie picked up her pace until she was within reach of Ian. She ran her hand across the broad expanse of his shoulders, leaving her hand to rest on his shoulder. "Ian?" she said softly.

Still, he didn't look up. Annie peeked around to see what he was doing. She saw him drawing on a large piece of paper. He was drawing a floor plan. As Annie watched, she realized it was the floor plan of the kennel. "What do you need that for?" she asked. "You know where they put the dogs, don't you?"

Ian began drawing in all the doors and windows on the plan. "Access," he whispered, his voice raspy.

Annie looked at him quizzically. His voice sounded so odd in the whisper. She leaned in closer to see his face. He turned to look at her, and Annie realized it wasn't Ian at all. The man who gazed at her was just a blur, his features shifting; it was like looking at an old video tape in slow motion. Anne backed away. "Who are you? What are you doing here?"

The man stood, looming over Annie. "Access," he whispered. "I had access. That's all I needed."

Annie turned and tried to run from the room, but her limbs were leaden. She seemed to barely move. No matter how much she struggled, she grew no closer to the door. *It's like running in slowly hardening amber*, she thought; then she realized that the air was turning golden and solid around her. She was literally trapped in amber. Her lungs strained to breathe, but only the thick amber poured in, clogging her throat.

Annie sat up sharply in bed, soaked in sweat and gasping for breath. Her panicky jump up had rolled Boots halfway across the bed, and the cat glared at her. "I'm sorry, Boots," Annie panted. "I had the most horrible dream."

She thought about the elements of the dream, including seeing the stranger at Ian's house. That's when the realization hit her. Ian was out of town, and Tartan was in the kennel. If the burglar wasn't going after Isabelle Murkleson's house, could he have gone after Ian's?

Annie jumped out of bed and began pulling on a pair of jeans. She had to get to Ian's house to check on it. She knew Ian would be upset if she went alone, so she picked up her phone and began dialing, apologizing into the handset even before the phone started to ring at Alice's house.

"Yes?" Alice answered, her voice amazingly alert for three in the morning.

"Alice, I'm so sorry to wake you," Annie said. "I had a bad dream, but it made me realize that Ian's house fits the burglary profile perfectly. I have to go check on it, and Ian would be upset if I went alone. Will you come with me?"

"Of course," Alice said. "Let me get some clothes on. I'll wait for you on my porch."

Annie flew through the rest of her dressing and hurried out the door. As she pulled up in front of Alice's house, she saw Jim standing on the porch beside Alice. Annie managed a smile as she noticed Jim was the least disheveled looking of the three of them, simply because he *always* looked a bit that way.

Alice and Jim quickly got into Annie's car.

"Hope you don't mind if I tag along," Jim said. "I don't like my favorite ladies facing danger alone. And Ian would not be happy if you got hurt while I stayed behind to snooze."

"Ian would be glad to know he worries you that much," Annie said. "But really, I'm grateful to you for coming along. The dream I had really shook me up, so I don't mind the company to check on Ian's house. It'll probably turn out to be nothing, but I couldn't just go back to sleep. I had to check."

"I don't blame you," Alice said, and Jim agreed.

Despite the empty roads, the drive seemed to take far longer than usual. Annie gripped the wheel tightly and said a silent prayer that Ian's house was OK. She jumped when she felt a warm hand on her shoulder.

"It'll be OK," Jim said. "We don't even know for sure that the kennel and the crimes are related."

"It would be quite a coincidence if they weren't," Alice said. "You pointed that out earlier."

"Yeah, it would, but the world is full of crazy coincidences," Jim said.

When they reached Ian's house, Annie pulled up the long driveway. She peered into the darkness around the house, looking for any sign of an intruder. "I don't see anything out of place," she said hopefully.

She parked, and they got out. They checked the front door and front windows, and everything seemed to be locked up tight. "Do you have a key?" Jim asked.

Annie nodded. "Ian gave me one when I was dog-sitting Tartan, but I'd like to check around the outside of the house first to see if there's any sign that someone has been here."

"Sounds good," Alice agreed as they stepped away from the front door.

They walked around to the back of the house, and Annie's hopeful feeling sank. The back door stood open a crack. Jim pulled a small flashlight out of his pocket and shone it on the keyhole. "Scratches," he said. "Someone picked the lock. Does the mayor have an alarm system?"

Annie shook her head. "He didn't when I was dog-sitting for him, and it seems like something he'd tell me about if he got one."

"We should go inside and see what's missing," Alice said.

Jim shook his head. "We should call the police and wait outside so we don't compromise evidence."

"Well, I'm surprised to hear you wanting to follow the rules," Alice said.

Jim grinned. "I don't want to face the mayor if I mess up the investigation."

Annie let the sound of her friends chatter wash over her as she pulled out her cellphone and called Chief Edwards. She wondered what it said about her that she had the chief of police on speed dial. Chief Edwards said he would leave immediately and cautioned Annie not to go into the house.

As soon as the chief hung up, she thought about calling Ian. Should she wake him when she really didn't know anything yet? Finally, she decided that she would want to know if the situation was reversed, so she dialed the number and listened to a sleepy voice mumble, "Hello?"

"Ian? It's Annie," she said, almost babbling. "I'm so sorry to wake you, but I'm at your house. I had a bad dream, and it made me worry about your house and the burglar, especially with Tartan in the kennel. At first it looked OK, and I was hoping it was just my overactive imagination, but your back door is open, and there are scratches on the lock."

"Hang up and call the police." Ian's voice had completely lost its sleepy softness.

"I did," Annie said. "I called Chief Edwards."

"Is he there?"

"Not yet, but he's on the way."

"I don't want you there alone," Ian said. "There's no way

of being sure the burglar is gone. I want you to get in your car and drive home. The chief can handle it from here."

"I'm not alone," Annie said reassuringly. "I'm here with Alice and Jim."

"Jim? Jim Parker?" Ian's tone sharpened. "Why is it that anytime you're in a crazy, dangerous place, he's there too?"

"That's not fair," Annie said. "I have been in plenty of crazy, dangerous places without Jim anywhere around. In fact, I had guns pointed at me before Alice ever even met Jim!"

Ian sighed. "That's not reassuring. Well, since you're not alone, could you go inside with the chief when he comes? You might be able to spot whatever is missing. But stay outside and stay together until the chief gets there."

"We will," Annie said.

"And call me again as soon as the chief is finished."

"I will."

"And be careful. And do not go in the house before the chief gets there, no matter how curious you get."

"We won't. In fact, it was Jim who insisted that we shouldn't go in the house," Annie said, hoping to soften Ian's feelings about Jim.

"OK, good," Ian said. "Oh, I have my laptop with me, so don't be surprised that it's not in my office."

"All right," Annie said.

"And be careful."

"You said that before."

"It's one of those things I say a lot to you," Ian said with another sigh. "I wish you didn't have such an instinct for getting into trouble, Annie Dawson."

"I don't go looking for trouble," Annie insisted.

"No," Ian agreed. "Not exactly. It's more like a magnetic attraction."

"I'll be careful," Annie assured him. "And I'll call the second the chief is done. I see headlights in the drive. That must be him."

"Stay on the phone until you're sure," Ian insisted.

Annie held the phone to her ear as the car pulled up the driveway. When it reached the house, the headlights angled away from her, and she could see beyond the dazzle of the light. It was Chief Edwards's car.

"It's the chief," Annie said. "I have to go."

"OK," Ian said. "Thanks, Annie."

Chief Edwards climbed out of the police cruiser and headed toward them. Annie noticed that the chief's sun-bleached hair looked nearly as wild as Jim's as the chief ran his fingers through it before putting on his cap. The chief was a tall man with a lumberjack's broad build, and he sported an unusual bit of beard stubble at that early hour of the morning. Despite the time, he seemed totally alert as he looked over the back door.

"Have you heard any sounds from inside?" he asked.

The trio shook their heads. "We haven't seen any cars either," Annie said.

"I expect the burglar is long gone," Chief Edwards said, "but you'd better wait out here while I secure the house, just to be sure."

Annie nodded and watched anxiously as the chief eased the back door open without touching any of the surfaces with his skin, and then slipped into the dark house.

Soon another police car pulled up, and the officers slipped into the house after the chief. Annie and the others anxiously waited outside. Jim eventually limped over to settle onto a wooden bench near the door. "I can walk better than I can stand around," Jim said. Alice took a seat beside him and held his hand.

That left Annie alone to watch the door and worry. Finally, the chief came back out and waved Annie forward. "You've been in Ian's house before, right?" he asked.

Annie nodded. "A number of times."

"I have too," Alice volunteered. "I've sold him some Divine Décor knickknacks a time or two."

The chief gave her a knowing smile. Alice didn't like to be left out of any adventure. "I'd like to limit the number of people walking the crime scene right now. Still, I'd like to know if Annie can spot anything missing."

"I'll try," Annie said.

They walked through the back mudroom and the kitchen. Clearly the thief had ignored those rooms entirely. As they passed through other rooms, Annie noticed a small flat-screen television was missing and a gaming system that Ian had bought to amuse his niece and nephew when they visited.

"We looked at the back-door lock when we first got here," Annie said as the chief was writing down the information about the gaming system. "There were scratches on the lock, and I happened to see the same scratches on the locks at Stony Point Kennel."

"You just happened to see that? We'll be dusting for prints, of course, though none of the previous robberies had any fingerprint evidence. We suspect the burglar wears gloves," Chief Edwards said, smiling slightly. "Anything else you've happened to notice?"

"Actually, yes," Annie said. "I've noticed that every victim, including Ian now, had pets in the kennel at the time of the robberies. It was really Alice who figured that out."

"That *is* interesting. I'll look into it, but you have to know that a lot of people in Stony Point have pets, and we only have the one kennel. Now, do you see anything else missing?"

"We should check Ian's den," Annie said. "I know he has a stereo in there."

She walked into the room with a shiver of déjà vu after her earlier dream. She was glad to find Ian's chair empty, though she hadn't really expected to find a faceless intruder there. Sadly, the space on his shelf where the stereo normally sat was empty as well. "The stereo is gone," she said. Her gaze swept over the room, and she noticed something else. "There's normally a small sculpture here on this table. Ian might have moved it, but if not, it was taken."

Chief Edwards nodded. "This thief seems to have quite a fondness for art. We'll check with Ian to be certain it wasn't moved."

"I can call him right now." Annie held up her phone. "I know he's up. I called when we were waiting for you."

"Of course you did," Chief Edwards said. "Fine. Please call now and ask about the missing items."

Annie dialed the phone, and Ian picked up before she even heard the first ring. "Are you OK?" Ian asked.

"Of course," Annie said. "I'm here with Chief Edwards. Your television and gaming system are missing, and so is the stereo from your den. I also noticed the little sculpture of the dancer is gone from your den, unless you moved it somewhere else."

"No, I never moved it," Ian said, his voice heavy. "I don't care about the electronics, but that sculpture was Arianna's favorite. I gave it to her after she saw it in a gallery in New York City. She loved it. Said it reminded her of herself when she was a girl and just learning to dance."

"Oh, Ian, I'm so sorry," Annie said.

"It was the first really big gift I ever gave Arianna," he said. "It was insured, of course."

"But insurance isn't enough sometimes," Annie said softly.

"No," Ian agreed. "Some things are irreplaceable." He took a deep breath. "I will be coming home right away. I've already packed, and so has Todd."

"Did you get the situation with the boat settled?" Annie asked.

"No, but I don't really care about it now. I'll see you soon, Annie. You better let me talk to the chief."

Annie handed her phone over to Chief Edwards, and she looked around the room again, her dream making everything look a bit more sinister. Who was breaking into the homes in Stony Point? Was there any chance that she and Alice could find the burglar in time to get Ian's sculpture back? Annie hoped so, to the bottom of her heart.

Since it was full daylight by the time the chief was done with the house, Annie drove over to The Cup & Saucer with Alice and Jim for some breakfast and to plan their next step in the investigation.

Peggy greeted them at the door with a bright smile and a spring in her step. "I'm always happy to see three of my favorite customers."

"I don't know how I managed to make it to favorite status," Jim said as he followed her to a table. "I don't tip that much."

"Sometimes it's the company you keep," Peggy said with a sassy grin, "not the money you put on the table. I happen to approve of the company you keep."

"Thank you," Alice said, slipping her arm through Jim's. "As the company he keeps, I'm glad to hear it."

They settled at a table near the large front windows. Jim ordered bacon and eggs and pancakes. Alice raised an eyebrow as he placed the large order. "Why is it that if I ate that way, I'd swell up like a tick, but you eat like that all the time and stay the same size?"

Jim shrugged. "No one ever said life was fair, but if you do decide to swell up like a tick, I'll still adore you."

"Right, sure you will," Alice said.

"More to love," he said before taking a sip from his coffee mug. "I have to admit, I needed this coffee. I'm getting too old for such short nights."

"I'm sorry," Annie said. "I shouldn't have bothered you two, but I guess I was scared to go out alone. The nightmare I had left me jumpy."

Alice leaned over to pat Annie's arm. "I'm glad you called. I would have yelled at you if you hadn't. And I can just imagine what Ian would have said."

Annie nodded. Ian constantly thought she took too many chances. She sighed. "I feel so bad about the break-in. I should have thought of Ian's house earlier when we found out the Murkleson woman was a bust."

"You know, I've been thinking about her," Jim said.

"I'll bet," Alice said, frowning slightly. "You sure you didn't see her in her altogether?"

"I only have eyes for you, Red," Jim said. "No, I've been thinking about her as a suspect. She puts the dog into the kennel regularly when she has a man at her house. Maybe the guy is visiting for more than just a good time? Maybe they're robbing houses together. It wouldn't be the first time a smart man led a bored rich girl astray."

"Oh, that's devious," Alice said. "I like how your mind works."

"It sounds like it would be helpful to know if Ms. Murkleson's little dog was in the kennel during all of the robberies," Annie said.

"Yep," Jim agreed. "I would say that would be very helpful indeed."

When their food arrived, Annie picked at a warm blueberry muffin as Alice teased Jim about his eating habits, though she also stole a bite or two of his pancakes. Their cheerful teasing made Annie miss Ian all the more. And missing Ian made her feel guilty. And feeling guilty made her stomach hurt. So she barely ate any of the muffin as she sipped tea.

"You're not eating," Alice finally noticed. "You're not still feeling sick?"

Annie shook her head. "No, I'm still feeling guilty."

"You know Ian isn't going to blame you," Alice said. "You didn't rob his house. The best thing we can do is to figure out who the bad guys are here. Then maybe we can get Ian's stuff back."

Jim tossed his napkin on the table and looked at his watch. "I think the next step in this mystery is heading back to the kennel. Do you know what time it opens?"

Annie looked at her own watch. "Not for another hour."

"Might be worth driving over early," Jim said. "Just to see what kind of action goes on when the place is closed."

Alice took a last sip of her coffee. "I'm ready, though Annie hasn't done much more than rough up that muffin."

"I'm full." Annie waved for Peggy, and the group quickly paid their bill. They headed out to the kennel in relative silence. Annie knew she did a terrible job of hiding her worries. Wayne had always said the story of everything she felt was plain on her face.

When they pulled up at the kennel, Margaret Freeman was peering under bushes near the front door. She straightened up to look when Annie pulled up.

"Annie," she said. "It's a bit early in the morning if you're dropping off Boots."

Annie shook her head as an idea came to her. "I came by to check on Tartan. I know it's silly, but Ian's house was robbed last night, and I'll just feel better if I can cuddle Tartan a little."

Margaret looked shocked. "Oh, that's horrible. I'm surprised a burglar can get away with so many robberies around here. To be honest, folks are almost too attentive to what goes on with the neighbors. Surely, someone is going to see this thief at work eventually. I just hope it's soon."

"That's a good point," Jim said. "It *is* surprising that no one has seen this housebreaker."

"Well, Stony Point is a fishing town," Alice said. "In general, people tend to go to bed early. It could simply be that no one is up that late."

"Maybe," Jim agreed reluctantly.

Margaret turned to Jim with polite interest, and Alice quickly introduced them. "Oh, I believe we have one of your books," Margaret said. "My husband is a bit of a photography buff. He'll be thrilled to meet you."

"Wow, a fan," Jim said.

"You have lots of fans around here," Alice said.

Jim laughed and leaned close to whisper something in Alice's ear. Annie was surprised to see her friend's cheeks color slightly. Alice wasn't like Annie. She didn't blush over everything.

Annie cleared her throat, drawing Margaret's attention back to her. "May I see Tartan? I know it's early, and I'm being silly, but I really would appreciate it."

"Of course," Margaret said. "Come on around, and we'll go in the back. I left it unlocked."

As they trailed along behind Margaret, Alice spoke, "Did you lose something in the front bushes?"

"I'm not sure where we lost it," Margaret said. "But we came up one key short a couple of days ago. Every once in a while I think of a new place to look."

"Have you changed the locks?" Jim asked.

Margaret shook her head. "No, it's not worth the expense. I'm sure someone just misplaced it. We can be a forgetful bunch around here. I would mostly like to find it so I know none of our clients ate it." She suddenly stopped and turned around. "Not that we don't take care to keep things like that from getting into the animal cages. Our staff is very conscientious about the animals."

"I'm sure they are," Annie said soothingly. "Still, it might be a good idea to change the locks."

"I don't think we have much risk of a break-in," Margaret said. "Can you imagine someone sneaking in with all the dogs? They start barking if a raccoon *thinks* about walking around the building, so they'd certainly let us know if someone was breaking in."

"Do they wake you often?" Annie asked. "Barking at stray animals outside?"

"More times than I'd like. Maynard has learned to sleep through the barking, and it has gotten better since we in-stalled all the additional soundproofing. Really, I just like to complain. I probably don't get up more than once or twice a week anymore."

"Do you always go check to see what's making them bark?"

"I used to, but then I realized I'd be up and down all night. It was making me very cranky during the day. Plus, if the dogs thought I'd come running as soon as they barked, they would never stop."

Annie nodded. What Margaret said made perfect sense, but it also meant the dogs weren't much of a deterrent. A clever, sneaky thief could let himself in the back door, check out the customer roster, and sneak back out without being spotted, even if Margaret did come downstairs for a cursory search. Annie felt more and more confident that the kennel was the key to the mystery—it was either someone working at the kennel or someone with frequent access.

They finally reached the door that led to the indoor dog kennels. As expected, the dogs began making quite a lot of noise as they walked in. Annie spotted Tartan, and the lively schnauzer launched himself at Annie as soon as Margaret opened his cage.

Annie was surprised at just how comforting it was to hug the wriggling dog as he licked her chin. Jim and Alice waited patiently near the dog cages. Alice spoke to several of the dogs and was rewarded with wagging tails.

"I see Paris is still here," Alice said as she pointed at the small dog's cage.

"Yes, he is," Margaret said. "I wouldn't put my fingers too close to the cage though. Paris can be a biter."

"Most Pomeranians can be," Alice said mildly. "And he's probably out of sorts from being away from home."

"As often as he's been in here lately, this probably feels more like home than his own."

Annie couldn't think of any subtle way to ask her question, so she simply decided to be open. "Margaret, has Paris been in the kennel during all the burglaries in Stony Point?"

Margaret looked surprised by the question. "I don't know," she said. "Maybe. He's been here a lot. That's certainly an odd question."

"Chief Edwards told me he's going to come by and ask you some questions. There are some eerie coincidences between pets in the kennel and the break-ins," Annie said. "Could you check on those dates? If it happens that Paris has been here during every burglary, could you please tell the chief?"

"I still don't understand," Margaret said, "but I'll do as you ask."

"Thanks," Annie said.

"Hey, is Jensen at work today?" Alice asked.

"Oh, do you know Jensen?" Margaret asked, her face brightening from its earlier confusion. "He's such a help around here. He's not working today though. He called in sick."

"Oh, is he sick a lot?" Alice asked.

"Not usually, though he's missed quite a bit of work lately," Margaret said. "You know, with so many new viruses going around, it's a wonder we don't spend half our time in bed sick, especially since we deal with the public. And it's so hard to sort out which foods are good for my immune system and which are certain to kill me. They seem to change constantly."

"That's why I just eat whatever I want," Jim said. "I figure, who wants to live forever?"

"I'd just as soon you made it through a few more years," Alice said, giving him a friendly push.

Tartan had finally gotten enough petting from Annie to sit calmly beside her. "Thank you so much for letting me see Tartan. It made me feel much better."

"I can tell," Margaret said. "You looked so worried when you got here. Do tell Ian that I'm so sorry about his home."

Annie nodded. "He should be by to pick up Tartan sometime today. I know he's cut short his trip to come home."

Margaret nodded, and the group bid their farewells. As

they walked to the car, Alice said, "Well that trip was interesting. We learned they lost a key to the kennel. And that Jensen has missed a lot of work lately."

"I still hate to convict the kid based on skipping work," Jim said. "Or on his ability to pick locks. I've done a bit of both in my time."

"I'm not convicting him," Alice said. "But he's a person of interest, for sure."

"As is Isabelle Murkleson," Annie said. "I'll be interested to find out if the dates of Paris's kennel visits match the burglaries."

"Will Chief Edwards share that kind of information with you?" Jim asked in surprise.

"Maybe not with me," Annie admitted. "But possibly with Ian."

"Ah, the mayor," Jim said. "Well, looks like we're at an impasse until he gets home."

"I do think we have one more stop we could try," Alice said. "Jensen's house."

"We don't have his address," Annie said.

"Nope, so I think we need to put the Hook and Needle Club on it," Alice said. "I'll call Mary Beth, and I expect we'll have it within the hour."

"Time to call out the sleuths," Jim said.

They leaned against Annie's car as Alice made the call. When Alice hung up, she smiled. "They'll call me back as soon as they have it."

"In the meantime, I'd like to look at the scratches on the lock," Jim said. "Now that I've seen the ones on Ian's door, I'd just like to take a look at the ones here."

"These folks are going to think we love this kennel," Annie said as they trooped back around the building. When they got to the back door, Jim bent to look at the lock. Finally he looked up and said, "Yep, this lock's been picked, and more than once. There are scratches on top of scratches on there. Some have been weathered more than others, but I can't tell if any are really fresh."

"Margaret said a key had gone missing," Alice said. "Maybe the crook stole the key and doesn't have to pick the lock anymore."

"That's very interesting," Annie said. "But it doesn't look really good for Jensen since he didn't have more than one good reason to pick the lock."

"All I can tell is that the lock's been picked more than once," Jim said, "not whether it was always picked by the same person."

"Still, a picked lock means a break-in," Alice insisted.

They turned back the way they'd come. When they turned the corner on the building, they walked right up on Margaret in an affectionate embrace with her husband. "Oh, my," Annie said. "Excuse me. I'm so sorry."

Margaret laughed, but Maynard's cheeks pinked slightly. "That's OK. I didn't know you were still here. We were just celebrating."

"Celebrating?" Annie asked.

"We've managed a new record," Maynard answered. "It's been over two full weeks since Bryan Norman has complained about the kennel. No calls about the noise. No rude notes about the smell. Nothing."

"Honestly, I'd have wondered if he'd just keeled over in

his yard from meanness, except that I saw him last night," Margaret said.

"You did?" Jim asked.

She nodded. "I was running the dogs around the backyard a couple times before putting them in for the night, and I saw Bryan hanging around the edge of his property watching me. I waved."

"Did he wave back?" Jim asked.

She chuckled. "No, but he didn't shake his fist, so I figured that was almost as good as a wave."

"I have to admit," Maynard said, "it'll be a big relief if the complaints are done for good."

Margaret gave him a quick hug. "It sure will be."

Annie and her friends bid the cheerful couple goodbye and headed for the car. "So much for the Stony Point gossip mill," Alice said. "Those two sure didn't look on the edge of divorce."

"Sounds like this neighbor has been causing them some stress though," Jim said.

"I wonder why he stopped?" Annie mused.

"The soundproofing must have worked," Alice said.

Annie shook her head. "No, when they put it in, he just switched to complaining about the smell—remember? I wonder what has him suddenly not complaining at all."

Jim perked up. "Maybe someone threatened him?"

"Now that's another interesting theory," Alice said.

"I'm full of them."

Alice laughed. "That's the truth."

— 8 —

As Annie drove away from the kennel, she said, "Where to now?"

"Let's go to A Stitch in Time," Alice said. "We can see the Stony Point Intelligence Network in action."

"I might part company with you at the door," Jim said. "There's too much estrogen in the air when a gossip network really gets going. I'll just head down to the diner and have some more coffee and maybe some pie."

"After that breakfast you ate?" Alice asked.

"That was almost two hours ago, and pie is full of fruit. It's practically health food."

They were still talking about the relative health benefits of pie when Annie pulled into a parking space in front of A Stitch in Time. Jim walked them to the door of the shop, and then kissed Alice on the cheek and headed toward the diner with a bit of a jaunty swagger in his uneven gait.

"So," Annie said when Jim was out of hearing. "Has he popped the question?"

Alice shook her head. "Not *the* question. He has popped *a* question. He wants me to travel with him while he shoots this new book."

Annie raised her eyebrows in surprise. "All over the world?"

"All over the world. He figures it'll take about a year."

"I'll miss you," Annie said.

Alice shook her head. "I haven't said I'll go. How can I just up and leave my business and my home for a year? I'm not made of money, and I have a mortgage now."

"Have you brought that up with Jim?" Annie asked.

"Not this time," Alice said. "Though I have told him I can't just dash off with him whenever he shows up. And I've told him why. If I'm not here selling, there's no money coming in."

"Did he have anything to say to that?"

Alice sighed. "Of course. With his lifestyle, he doesn't spend much money. He has a lot saved. He offered to help me, but I *like* taking care of myself."

"Did you tell him that?"

"Yes. And he said he understands. He said he likes my independent nature. But then he shows up asking me to drop everything and spend a year traveling all over the world. Why would he even ask if he really understood?"

Annie smiled. "Because he loves you and doesn't want to be away from you for a year?"

"It's not that easy."

"Here's a thought," Annie said. "You could marry him, and then you won't feel so bad if your house payments are still made while you're traveling the world with your husband."

"Sure, good plan," Alice said, wryly. "We'll have a double wedding. Me and Jim, you and Ian."

"Don't even joke about that," Annie said in alarm.

Alice opened her mouth to say something else, but suddenly the door to A Stitch in Time flew open, making both women jump.

"Are you two coming in?" Mary Beth asked. "The curiosity over what you're talking about is killing us."

"And Mary Beth is terrible at reading lips," Kate added from where she stood behind Mary Beth.

"Kate isn't any better. I thought you were talking about going to the police over that case," Mary Beth said. "Which makes sense. Kate thought you were talking about getting married, which is crazy. Though a certain mayor we know could be thinking along those lines. You never know."

"You never know," Alice agreed.

"I know! Ian and I are nowhere near ready to talk marriage," Annie said firmly, feeling heat flood into her cheeks. All she needed was for gossip to get back to Ian that she'd been talking about their wedding!

"As long as you let *us* know when the big moment happens," Mary Beth said.

"So, how goes the hunt for Jensen's address?" Alice asked, generously changing the subject.

"Well, Gwen had no idea," Mary Beth said. "She'd never heard of him. Peggy recognized the name, but she didn't know where he lives either. But we did find a surprising source. We're just waiting for the address."

Annie and Alice both looked at her expectantly, but Mary Beth just gestured toward Kate. "Well, Peggy told us that Jensen is just a couple years older than Vanessa," Kate said. "And Vanessa does seem to pay attention to boys. So I texted her, and she texted back that she did know that name and that Jensen's younger brother was in her summer improv class with her. She's going to ask him the address since that's where she is today."

"Second-generation grapevine," Alice said. "I love it."

"The only problem is that Vanessa is only allowed to use her cellphone during lunch or after the program is over for the day," Kate said, "so we may be waiting a while."

Annie and Alice settled into the comfy chairs where the Hook and Needle Club met once a week. It felt good to settle into the overstuffed chair, and Annie was reminded that she was probably pushing a little too hard considering she was still recovering from her cold.

"Improv," Annie said. "Is that like acting? That must be the 'hot' summer activity. My grandchildren were at an acting camp last Sunday."

"It's like acting," Kate said. "Only they make up everything for their scenes at the spur of the moment. The acting bug only bit Vanessa after she met Logan. I'm hoping it's a phase."

"Well, it's good for young people to try a lot of different things," Annie said.

"I know," Kate agreed. "And I try to be supportive, but I have to admit, I would rather she'd try things that can lead to regular employment in drug-free environments."

"Vanessa has a level head on her shoulders," Mary Beth said firmly. "I don't think you have to worry about her too much."

"I don't have a choice," Kate said. "I'm a mom."

Annie leaned back in her chair and closed her eyes for a moment as her friends talked. She reminded herself not to push her body too hard.

"Can I get you both some tea?" Mary Beth asked. "I have some nice chai."

Annie's eyes flicked open. "That would be wonderful," she said, allowing her leaden eyelids to fall again. She heard Alice hop back out of the chair beside her. Annie wasn't overly surprised. Alice often had trouble just sitting unless she had something to keep herself occupied.

"Is this a new design?" Alice asked. Annie opened her eyes. Alice was looking over a beautiful crochet sweater set. The cardigan part of the set was done in filet crochet with flower designs. The tank underneath was solid with a delicate trim that looked like flowers.

"Yes," Kate said. "I have been fascinated by filet crochet lately. It's so mathematical in its approach with the grid."

Alice nodded. "It reminds me a little of cross-stitch too. Probably for the same reason—the grid you use to plan the design or follow the pattern."

"Have you ever done any filet crochet?" Kate asked Annie.

"Only small things," Annie admitted. "I tend to get lost in the pattern. It's the same reason I don't do crossstitch, but I did find a darling baby blanket that uses filet on some of the blocks. I thought I'd try my hand at it again. I just hope my cute bunnies and kittens don't end up looking like blobs. Actually, I wrote down the yarn I need for the project. I should go ahead and buy it while I'm here." She rummaged in her purse to get the notebook.

"Ah, a sale," Mary Beth said as she strode over to Annie. "That's what I like to hear. Oh yes, I have some of this. You sit, I'll get it."

Annie happily leaned back into the chair with a sigh. "I just hope I'm not fooling myself, thinking I can handle this kind of pattern."

Alice laughed. "It helps to make little notes on the pattern to keep track of where you are. If it's like cross-stitch, it just takes concentration. That's the thing I like about cross-stitch."

"That's the great thing about crafts," Mary Beth said as she carried the yarn over to Annie. "There's something for everyone if you just keep trying new things."

"I like the way a craft gives you a framework for testing your own talents and artistry," Kate said.

"Ah, spoken like a true artist," Mary Beth agreed. The whistle of her electric teakettle pulled Mary Beth away from the group. "I'll get the tea for you two." She collected the mugs and poured steaming water into them.

"Speaking of artists," Annie said, "did Stella have any ideas of more places we could check to track down some of the stolen art?"

Mary Beth returned with mugs of tea, handing them to Annie and Alice. "Stella says she is 'hardly in a position to know anyone who fences stolen goods,'" she said, copying Stella's slightly superior tone perfectly.

"No, of course not," Annie said.

"Still, it's too bad," Alice added. "We're not drowning in art contacts. I wonder if Ian might know anyone. He seems to know a lot of people in Stony Point and outside Stony Point too."

"I'll ask him when he gets back," Annie said. "Since we're going to be waiting a while, do you think you should join Jim?" Annie asked.

"Jim?" Mary Beth echoed. "Jim Parker is in town? How nice. You should make him come by and see us."

"He thinks the shop is too girlie," Alice said.

Mary Beth snorted. "What does he think, he'll catch a bad case of pink or something?"

Alice shrugged. "I've never pretended I actually understand men."

"You should go get him," Mary Beth insisted. "Drag him down here so we can chat with him."

Alice raised one eyebrow as she looked at Mary Beth. Annie suspected Alice wasn't totally sure it was in her best interest for Mary Beth to grill her friend. Mary Beth was prone to asking embarrassing questions whenever she suspected romance.

The question became moot when Kate's cellphone made an odd noise. She looked at it in surprise. "It's Vanessa. She's hiding out in the bathroom to text."

"Does she have the address?" Annie asked.

Kate nodded, stepping over to the counter to scribble the address on the back of a business card. "Here you go." She handed over the card, adding, "Vanessa says he lives alone."

Alice glanced down at the card. "I don't go out this way much, but I know where the road is. Thanks, Kate, and thank Vanessa for me."

"Hey, if this catches the person who robbed Ian and the other people, that's all that matters," Kate said, and Mary Beth nodded emphatically.

Annie paid for the yarn for her project and tucked it into her purse. Then she and Alice collected Jim from the diner where he was shamelessly flirting with Peggy. As they walked out of the diner, Alice poked him. "One of these days you're going to flirt with the wrong lady and get roughed up by a husband."

Jim grinned mischievously. "You know Peggy doesn't take me seriously, and I've met her husband. Wally's a great guy. He's not worried about an old dog with fake legs."

Alice gave him another frown. "You're lucky *I* don't take you seriously."

"With you," he said, "I'm always serious about the important stuff."

"Sure."

The ride out to Jensen's house took them several miles from the center of town. The road was spotted with potholes that challenged Annie's driving skills. "This road is terrible," she complained.

"It's the winters," Alice said. "The snow and ice and plows are rough on the paved roads, and repairs tend to start with the main roads. They get to places like this *whenever*."

Stony Point had lots of beautiful trees throughout, but the land along the sides of the gravel road was particularly thick with growth. It came as some surprise when the thick growth suddenly stopped, and they found themselves driving by a battered trailer park.

"Oh, my," Annie said. "I didn't know they even had trailer parks around here."

"I would be willing to guess that we crossed out of the city limits quite a ways back," Alice said. "That happens a lot up here. Towns don't want trailer parks, so they pop up in the odd spots right where town lines end."

"But these trailers look awful," Annie said. "I think some of them are older than me."

"I've seen worse," Jim said. "I've lived in worse."

Since the mailboxes were all in a single spot, piled on top of one another, it was difficult to find which trailer was Jensen's. They drove slowly up the gravel road that looped between the small lots. Then Alice yelped and pointed. "There, look."

A small trailer that had once been uniformly silver but now shared its outer color with rust sat slightly off level on cinderblocks. A large number five was spray-painted on the side.

"If the kid's living there," Jim said, "he's not spent any ill-gotten gains on himself."

Jensen opened the door after Jim pounded on it for a while. The young man looked terrible. His eyes were runny, and his nose looked raw. He blinked at them miserably. "Can I help you?"

"Are you all right?" Alice asked.

Jensen shook his head. "Not really. I'm not sick; it's just my allergies. I'm just out of my meds and was a little strapped for cash."

Annie looked at the young man in dismay. "Don't they pay you at the kennel?"

The young man stiffened. "They pay just fine. And I'm lucky to have the work. I just have expenses. Do you want something?"

"We met at the kennel," Annie said soothingly. "I'm not sure if you remember. I'm Annie Dawson, and you met Alice as well. And this is Jim Parker. We were hoping to talk to you a little bit about the kennel."

"Yeah," Jim said. "We want to talk about the lock on the kennel. I saw it. It's been picked a bunch of times, but the owner only remembers you doing it once."

Jensen nodded, looking confused. "I did just pick it the one time. Why would anyone do it again?"

"It's kind of complicated," Annie said gently. "Jensen, may we come in?"

He looked behind him, and then he shrugged. "The place is a mess. I don't know if you ladies really want to be in here, but you can come in if you want." He shuffled backward to let them in.

The trailer was small and tight, one of those spaces that functions best when there's a place for everything and everything is in its place. As they walked in, they knew *nothing* was in its place. The trailer looked like it had been ransacked. Used tissues littered the floor amongst dirty laundry. The small sink was piled with dishes.

"Sorry," Jensen said. "When I'm not feeling well, I'm kind of a pig."

"Jensen," Annie said gently, "what do you take for your allergies? I would be glad to go and get the prescription filled."

"Oh, you don't have to do that, ma'am," Jensen said. "After a day or so at home, I'll feel better. I'm allergic to pet dander." He shrugged sheepishly. "I guess I didn't pick the best job."

"Considering what it does to you, why do you work for the kennel?" Alice asked.

Jensen shrugged. "'Cause they'll have me. At least, that's why I started there. But I like the job. Mr. and Mrs. Freeman have been really good to me. And I like the animals." He smiled again. "Even if they do make me sneeze and itch."

"Look, hand over the prescription," Jim said. "There's no reason to be miserable when you can feel better and get back to work sooner." He turned to Annie. "If you don't mind letting me use your car, I can get it."

Annie nodded and handed him the keys. After a stern look, Jensen handed over the empty prescription bottle to be filled. "Walk out with me," Jim said to Alice. "You can give me directions to the nearest pharmacy."

Alice and Jim left the trailer, and Annie did find it a little easier to be inside with fewer people, though the heat and smell of sweat were oppressive. "Let me pick up in here a little for you," Annie said. "You'll feel better if you're less ... higgledy-piggledy."

"Oh, no, ma'am," Jensen said in alarm. "I'd feel terrible about a nice lady like you picking through my mess." He quickly shoved a pile of clothes from the seat of a folding chair and gestured toward it. "Please, sit down."

Annie nodded, though the urge at least to do the dishes nagged at her. "Margaret Freeman said you've missed a fair bit of work lately."

Jensen shrugged. "I don't have insurance because I don't work full time. So sometimes it's hard to buy my allergy meds. I'll be fine for days, but then it hits me really hard."

Annie looked around the trailer. "It doesn't seem as though this should be very expensive to rent."

"It's not bad," he said. "I pay by the week. And my motorcycle is good on gas, but I try to give some money to my mom too. I've still got a brother and sister at home."

"That's good of you."

He shrugged and ducked his head shyly. "It's no big deal. It's my *mom*, you know."

Annie nodded. "Have you heard about the burglaries around town?"

Jensen looked up sharply, narrowing his eyes. "Yeah?"

"All the people who've been robbed had pets in the kennel," Annie said.

"So you thought it must be the juvenile delinquent who works there," Jensen said.

Annie smiled slightly. "You actually weren't our first suspect, but I do think the robberies are linked to the kennel. Someone has been breaking in, and I think they've done it to find out who has pets in the kennel."

"It wasn't me," he said, crossing his arms and scowling.

"I know," Annie said. "You're clearly not living the life of a successful burglar. And a motorcycle is not exactly an ideal burglary get-away vehicle. Plus, Ian Butler's house was broken into last night, and you clearly have been here ... using a lot of tissues."

"But you thought it *might* have been me," he grumbled.

"We thought we should ask you some questions," she said. "It's not good that the kennel may have been used to plan burglaries. Do you have any ideas about who might be involved?"

"Well, it wasn't Mr. or Mrs. Freeman," he insisted. "They wouldn't have to pick the kennel lock. They live there. And it wasn't Marcie. She adores her aunt and uncle. She wouldn't do anything to get them in trouble. Plus, she's a relative so she wouldn't need to pick the lock either. She has a key. I have one too. Well, I did. I lost it a couple days ago, and I'm still looking for it."

Annie looked around the tissue-covered floor. *Good luck with that*, she thought.

"Is there anyone you can think of with a pet in the kennel lately who hasn't been robbed?" Annie asked. "Anyone clearly successful or affluent?"

"Well, I don't know if Mrs. Freeman would want me talking about clients."

Annie nodded. "It's not going to be good for the kennel if these robberies keep going on and eventually get linked in people's minds with the kennel."

"Well, maybe Ms. Murkleson. That little Pomeranian of hers is in the kennel all the time lately," he said. "She hasn't been robbed, and even I can tell she must have scads of money."

Again Annie nodded. A lot of questions kept turning back to Isabelle Murkleson. Had she been home every time the dog was in the kennel? If so, why would anyone go to the expense of putting such a little dog in the kennel just because she was having an overnight guest?

"It would be helpful if we knew if the Pomeranian was in the kennel during every break-in," Annie said.

"I could check," Jensen said. "I mean, since I'll have my allergy meds, I'll be able to go back to work. And I could check and let you know. The kennel is a great place to work, and I don't want Mr. and Mrs. Freeman to have any trouble."

Annie smiled at the boy. "I think they're lucky to have you. And now I have to ask one more favor."

"Anything."

"I'd really like to wash your dishes," Annie said. "It's the mom in me. Really, I'll feel better."

Jensen blushed but nodded. "OK, Mrs. Dawson. And I'll pick up out here."

When Alice came back into the trailer, she joined in the general cleanup. The trailer looked much better by the time Jim came back with the medicine. "I should have known you two couldn't leave a guy in his nice comfortable mess," Jim said as he looked over the small trailer.

"It's easier to heal in a clean room," Alice insisted.

Jim just shook his head. "Are we done grilling and cleaning?"

Annie said they were. Jensen said he'd call as soon as he knew anything about the kennel that could help with the investigation. He seemed to have gotten quite caught up in the idea of playing detective once he had time to think about it—especially now that he knew neither Margaret nor Maynard were really a suspect.

"Where to now?" Jim asked as he headed for the driver's side of Annie's car.

"Oh, you're the driver now?" Alice asked.

"You know me, Red," he said. "I like to be in control."

She just shook her head, though a smile crept through her stern expression. "We probably should head home. Annie looks like she could use a nap."

"I *am* a little tired," Annie admitted.

"Well, morning came kind of early today," Jim said as they climbed into the car.

Annie agreed. Morning had come early and brought with it such a heartbreaking robbery. As she sat sank into the backseat, she wondered when Ian would be home and how he was feeling. She knew the sense of violation that came from any break-in—but this time the thief had taken something Ian valued deeply. Annie hoped he was doing OK.

~ 9 ~

Annie was glad to see Grey Gables slip into view. She was tired and was seriously in need of a nap.

"Thanks for driving," she told Jim as he handed her the keys in her driveway. "I was nearly falling asleep in the backseat."

"I wouldn't mind a nap myself," Jim said, casting a sassy glance at Alice. "Unless Red can come up with something more entertaining."

"Sure, you can help me catch up on my bookkeeping," Alice said.

"Party pooper," he grumbled.

Annie just laughed and waved at her friends as they crossed the yard. As usual, Boots greeted her at the door with complaints about having been left alone. Annie reached down to scoop up the cat, but Boots sniffed her hands and backed away. "What's the matter?" Annie asked, and then she remembered. But her visit to the kennel was several hours and several hand washings ago, not to mention the fact she'd washed a sink load of dishes. "You can't tell me you still smell Tartan."

Boots just lashed her tail and glared at Annie.

"He's a very nice dog."

Boots offered only a squinty glare.

"OK, suit yourself," Annie said. "But I'm going to go take a nap, and we both know you can't resist that."

Annie decided to pass on another cramped nap on the couch. It reminded her too much of the recent feverish days. Instead, she grabbed the afghan from the couch and carried it to her bedroom. She curled up on the neatly made bed and was asleep in minutes.

As she slept, her subconscious took her on another strange trip, clearly caused by her concerns about the burglaries. She found herself running through the kennel, looking for someone. She wasn't sure who it was she needed to find, but she felt more and more frantic as she raced through endless empty hallways. She continued to run, panting until she leaned against a wall, struggling for breath. It felt like a weight laid on her chest. Then the weight on her chest grew thorns, digging into her skin.

Annie woke with a start to find Boots peering down into her face from her perch on Annie's chest. "No wonder I was having nightmares," she complained as she lifted the cat off.

Sitting up, she realized she heard the doorbell. She got up and padded through the house in her stocking feet. When she opened the door, she saw Ian smiling down at her. "Did I catch you in a nap?"

"How can you tell?" Annie asked.

"I had to ring the bell for quite a while," he said, counting reasons off on his fingers. "You don't normally walk around in socks. And though your hairstyle is quite fetching, it's unusual for you."

Annie's eyes widened in alarm as her hands flew to her head. She felt hair sticking up in several places. "Oh my."

"Don't worry about it," Ian said as he stepped closer

and wrapped his arms around her. "I'm just extremely glad to see you."

Annie was mildly surprised by both the gesture and the length of time Ian held her. "Are you OK?" she asked.

He gently released her. "I just came from the house. It caught me by surprise, just how upsetting I found it to see my house violated. And losing that little sculpture ..." He paused and shook his head. "It's not really like losing her again, but it's definitely revisiting the pain."

"Have you talked to Chief Edwards?"

He nodded. "He couldn't offer a lot of hope."

"Several of the break-ins have involved stolen art," Annie said. "I wonder if that might be key to tracking the pieces down. Art certainly can't be as easy to get rid of as electronics." Annie sighed. "Stella is the only person we know with any ties to the art community, but she couldn't find anything."

Ian frowned. "I imagine that the sort of friends Stella has wouldn't be trafficking in stolen goods."

"That's basically what she said, only I imagine her voice was more disapproving."

"What if the thief is taking the art to the same place people take electronics that they need to unload?" Ian mused.

"Which would be?"

"Pawn shops. We could check out some pawn shops. The police probably don't have time for that kind of time-consuming search, so we'd be helping out the investigation without stepping on any official toes."

Annie's eyes widened. "I've never been in a pawn shop in my life."

Ian grinned at her. "They can be a little seedy some-times, but just think of them as thrift shops with bars on the windows. You can find all sorts of things at a pawn shop, but I think most of their money comes from jewelry and electronics. And probably guns."

"So when do we start?" Annie asked.

"I don't think Friday night is a good time for taking a lady to pawn shops," Ian said. "I'll do an online search and make a list of all the pawn shops in driving range. We can start looking tomorrow."

"That sounds good," Annie said.

"Now, since it is Friday night," Ian said. "I thought I might ask a lovely lady if she'd like to have dinner with me."

"Lovely lady?" Annie echoed. "Is it anyone I know? Since I have bed hair and very rumpled clothes, you're either talk-ing about someone else or being astoundingly kind."

Ian leaned over and kissed her warmly. "You're always lovely to me, but I'll wait if you want to change and brush your hair."

"I might like to shower too," Annie said tentatively.

"No problem. I'm not starving yet, and I prefer to be here than at home right now. I can sit on your comfortable sofa and return some phone calls while you get ready."

"Thanks." Annie hurried off to get ready. When she got back to her bedroom, she passed a mirror and nearly shrieked. Then she laughed at her own horror. Ian had seen her soaked through from rain, covered in mud, and in all different levels of rumpled and stressed. If he hadn't run screaming yet, she guessed he must really like her.

After her shower, Annie dressed simply in jeans and

a light summer sweater. When she finally walked into the living room, she found Ian sitting on the sofa with Boots in his lap, absently stroking her while staring at his phone.

"All done," Annie said.

Ian looked up and smiled. "And well worth the wait. Alice called while you were in the shower. Jim had an idea for investigating someone named Murkleson?"

"Isabelle Murkleson," Annie said. "We think she and her new male friend *might* be involved in the thefts. She has had her dog in the kennel a lot lately. And it wouldn't be the first time a good-looking crook lured a woman into his plans." As soon as the words escaped her mouth, Annie felt her face grow red. Not long after she'd moved to Stony Point, a good-looking jewel thief had charmed Annie more than a little.

Ian nodded. "Should Chief Edwards know about this woman?"

"I don't know," Annie admitted. "Our suspicions are a little vague. One of the things I meant to ask you was if you'd check with the chief and see if he had learned if the lady's dog was in the kennel at the time of all the thefts."

"OK, hold on," Ian said. "Let me do that now."

Annie sat beside Ian on the sofa as he rang the chief. He spoke a few moments and then ended the call. "The chief says the dog spent a *lot* of time at the kennel. It also stayed when no one was robbed. The chief doesn't consider Ms. Murkleson a serious suspect."

"And she's probably not guilty," Annie said. "But she is unpleasant. Maybe we just like the idea of an obnoxious person being the guilty party."

"Stealing is obnoxious enough."

Annie nodded. "So, what's Jim's idea for learning more?"

"They're going to Ms. Murkleson's house tomorrow," Ian said. "Jim is going to pretend to be interested in doing a feature on her unusual home. I guess Alice is going along as camera carrier."

"That might work," Annie said. "Jim can charm information out of a rock."

Ian raised an eyebrow. "You find him charming?"

Annie smiled. "I do—but not nearly as charming as you. Plus, I think you're taller. And I've always preferred clean-shaven men."

"Nice save."

Ian drove them to Maplehurst Inn. Annie always enjoyed dining at the inn, where they were greeted so warmly that it was almost like having dinner with friends. Annie was also glad she'd had a chance to take a nap, as she was pretty sure she would have otherwise fallen asleep right in the middle of the meal.

As they walked into the dining room, Annie spotted Linda Hunter at the hostess stand.

"Are you playing dinner hostess tonight?" Ian asked.

Linda laughed. "It's the cost of being the owner. You have to be able to do anything in a pinch. Poor Kellie wasn't feeling well, so I sent her home."

"I know from recent experience what it's like to feel miserable. Tell her I hope she's feeling better soon," Annie said.

"I will." Linda turned to scan the room. "I have a table near the back. Is that OK for you, or would you prefer to wait a few minutes for something not so close to the kitchen?"

"That will be fine," Annie said. "I don't mind the back."

As soon as they settled into their seats, Ian reached across the table and took Annie's hands in his. She looked at him in surprise. He smiled back. "I was just thinking how much better I feel right now, sitting here with you. I know when I get home, I'll still have to face that someone broke in, but when I'm with you, it just doesn't seem to matter."

Since Ian wasn't usually quite so verbal about his feelings, Annie didn't quite know what to say. "I'm glad I can take your mind off it," she said finally. Then she realized how flatly unemotional that sounded.

"I have a question to ask you," Ian said.

Annie's thoughts immediately jumped to Alice's worry over Jim popping *the* question, and her teasing about a double wedding. *Ian isn't about to do something crazy, is he?* She froze and nodded.

"What are the chances we can get all the way through this mystery without you doing anything dangerous?" he asked. "Since I already have the stress of the break-in, I was just trying to figure how much more stress I might be under later."

"Oh," Annie said. "So far this has been totally danger-free. No threatening notes. No spooky phone calls. No one following my car. I think it's looking good."

"Well, just in case, I'd like you to promise no poking around in things on your own," Ian said. "I'm home now, and we can go together."

"I think I can promise that," Annie said. Normally she resisted when Ian started telling her what to do, but he seemed to be making an effort not to be bossy. And he'd just been through the break-in. She didn't want to make things harder for him.

By the relief on his face, Annie suspected he'd expected more resistance. "That makes me feel better," he said.

Annie caught sight of someone waving at her from over Ian's shoulder. She looked up and spotted Kate and Vanessa. Kate shot her a questioning look and pointed at Ian. Annie smiled and waved them over to the table.

"Hi," Kate said. "Are we intruding?"

"Not at all," Ian told them graciously. "Would you ladies like to join us?"

Again Kate shot a questioning glace toward Annie. "Please, do join us," Annie said.

As soon as they sat, the server rushed over with menus. Vanessa just laid hers on the table and leaned forward, her eyes bright with excitement. "So, what's up with the mystery?"

"Vanessa," Kate scolded. "Ian's house was broken into. Show a little tact."

Vanessa murmured an apology, but her eyes were still full of questions.

"That's perfectly all right," Ian said. "We were talking about the mystery before you joined us."

"Ian had a great idea of possibly tracking the sale of the art objects and electronics to pawn shops," Annie said. "We're going to visit the ones in driving range tomorrow."

"Oh, wow, that's so cool," Vanessa said. "Can I come?"

"No," Kate said. "You don't need to visit pawn shops."

"But I love that show about pawn shops on television," Vanessa said. "They have the coolest stuff in the world. Plus, it would be educational."

Kate shook her head as she pointedly looked at her menu. "You don't need that kind of education."

"Most pawn shops are not like that show," Ian told Vanessa. "And they're a little sad when you think about it. They collect things people have to give up when they fall on hard times."

"Oh," Vanessa said. "I hadn't thought of it that way."

"You've already been a big help with finding the address for Jensen," Annie said.

"Oh, right," Vanessa whispered. "His brother is really nice. You don't think Jensen is a burglar, do you? That would be awful."

"No, I don't suspect Jensen at all," Annie said. "I think he's a nice guy who seems very concerned about his family and his employers."

"Oh, I'm glad," Vanessa said as she sat back in her seat. "So did you guys do any online searching for the stolen stuff?"

"Online searching?" Annie said. "You mean people advertise stolen merchandise online?"

"Well, I'm sure they don't label it stolen," Vanessa said. "But if I wanted to get rid of some art, I'd use one of the online auction sites."

"Are there many of them?" Annie asked.

"Well, if you count little online stores, yeah," Vanessa said. "Hey, I could look. I mean, if you told me what any of the stuff looks like, I could look for it."

"OK, but don't go any further than looking," Ian said. He took a photo out of the inner pocket of his sport coat and passed it to Vanessa. "This is the photo of the sculpture that I took when we had the piece insured. When I emailed the photo to the chief, I printed one to carry around with me … just in case."

"Oh, it's pretty," Vanessa said. "Even without a face on the sculpture, you can tell that she's happy to be dancing."

Ian smiled. "Yes, that joy is one of the things my wife loved about it."

Vanessa pulled out her cellphone. "Let me snap a photo of this so I can look at it while I search. Do you think there are many of these figurines? Were they numbered or something so I can tell if I find this particular one?"

"It was one of a kind," Ian said.

"Oh. Wow, losing it must stink."

"It does."

That table sat in awkward silence for a moment, no one quite knowing what to say. Ian was visibly upset at losing the little dancer that his late wife had loved. With the group sitting silently, staring at one another, the server must have assumed they were ready to order. The young woman's cheerful bounce drew everyone out of the discomfort of the moment. Having to scramble to decide on what to order when only Kate had even opened a menu was a good distraction as well. Finally they had their orders in and could turn back to conversation.

Annie turned to Vanessa and asked, "So, how is Logan's play doing?"

Vanessa's eyes lit up. "Fantastic. He said the reviews have been great, and he's so glad for the chance to show off his singing and dancing. He loves stage work. He says it lets you really dwell inside your role, because you're not doing the story in pieces like you do with movies."

"I hadn't thought of that," Annie said. "It makes sense.

I'm glad Logan is enjoying it so much. He's a very nice young man."

Vanessa nodded. "And Logan's a great singer. Sometimes ..." she paused for a moment, her cheeks pinking; then she plunged on. "Sometimes he sings to me over the phone."

Annie turned a teasing smile toward Ian, "How come you never sing to me over the phone?"

"You've heard me sing," he said. "Are you sure you want that?"

"As I remember, everyone who heard you sing loved it," Annie said, "including me."

"I've only heard you sing a couple of times," Kate said, "and you're as good as Annie says. I'm surprised you don't sing solos at church."

"I do my singing," Ian said, "while holding my hymnbook and standing beside Annie. That's about all the attention I care for. People came up to me for weeks after that night of karaoke; I found it uncomfortable."

Annie could understand that. She'd skipped singing altogether that night, but she didn't have nearly the voice that Ian had. "Well, I was glad you sang that night. It was very touching."

Clearly uncomfortable, Ian quickly changed the subject. "Kate, are you still doing the column for the crochet magazine?"

"She is," Vanessa said eagerly, "and she even gets fan mail. It's so cool."

It seemed to be Kate's turn to blush then. Annie was glad Kate's crochet talents were being recognized beyond the tight confines of Stony Point, but she knew it could be hard on her shy friend to get that kind of attention.

"I enjoy doing the column," Kate said quietly. "It's nice to have that push to challenge me to create new things that are accessible to all skill levels."

Annie nodded. "I subscribed to the magazine when you started the column, and I've tried every single project you put in. They look so amazing, and I do find them challenging, but I've always been pleased by the result. To be honest, sometimes I wish you wrote the directions for all the projects I try."

Again conversation stopped as their server returned with salads and beverages. They spoke only casually for the rest of the dinner and managed to stay off topics that caused awkward pauses. Annie found the dinner restful after the stress of the burglaries, and she was glad to see Ian growing more relaxed as the evening passed.

Later, when he stood on her porch after driving her home, he smiled down at her. "Thank you for having dinner with me," he said. "I think it was just what I needed."

"I'm glad," Annie said. "I needed it too."

In the porch light, Ian's face was half in shadows, giving Annie a glimpse of the melancholy he'd shown earlier. She reached up and brushed her fingers across the shadowed side, as if to chase away the darkness. Ian trapped her hand against his cheek with his own.

"You're a wonder, Annie Dawson," he said.

He began to bend toward her, and Annie put a hand to his chest to stop him. He looked at her in surprise. "You forget I've been sick," she said. "I could still be contagious. The whole town would be mad at me if I made you sick."

"I'm willing to take the risk," he said.

"I think I have enough things to feel guilty about," she told him.

He raised his eyebrows. "Whatever could you feel guilty about?"

Annie sighed. "I knew there was a connection between pets in the kennel and the break-ins. I didn't have proof, but I still knew it. And I knew Tartan was in the kennel. We should have been watching your house, not that Murkleson woman. Or I should have offered to watch Tartan at your home. If I'd had any sense …."

Ian put a finger to her lips to shush her. "It is not your fault that my house was broken into." She started to protest but he shook his head. "It was not your fault. You aren't a burglar. You didn't steal anything from me. You are not to blame."

Annie sighed. "I still feel like I'm to blame."

Ian shook his head, smiling at her. "That's because you care. But it's still not right. I don't blame you, Annie." He bent quickly and brushed a quick kiss across her lips. "You need to go on to bed. I'll be over in the morning to start our pawn shop tour."

"You do take me to the nicest places, Mr. Mayor," she teased.

"All part of the job. Good night, Annie."

"Good night, Ian."

Annie headed into the house with a warm glow from the lovely evening. Her romantic mood was broken by Boots storming toward her, meowing insistently. Annie laughed. "Did I forget to feed you?"

Boots threaded through her legs, still meowing.

"Then we better get you fed," Annie said as she began walking carefully toward the kitchen while Boots did her best to trip her. "You know no one will be feeding you if you manage to trip and kill me."

Boots must have realized she'd herded Annie enough, because she dashed ahead to guard the food bowl until Annie arrived.

Once the cat was gobbling kibble, Annie yawned and headed back down the hall away from the kitchen. She needed to get to bed. She wanted to be alert for whatever Saturday might have in store.

~ 10 ~

Since Stony Point didn't have a pawn shop, Annie and Ian began their sleuthing with a drive to Storm Harbor, which had two. The first was in a pretty brick storefront with large glass windows. The dark awning that shaded the storefront had "Storm Harbor Pawn" printed across the front.

"It doesn't look quite like I expected," Annie said as they walked up the sidewalk toward the shop.

"What did you expect?"

"I don't know, something seedier, I guess," Annie said. "A place that looked dangerous."

"Storm Harbor still attracts quite a few tourists," Ian said. "I'm sure they wouldn't allow barred windows and neon signs right on Main Street—and I doubt that the shop needs that here anyway."

"That makes sense," Annie agreed as she peered in the windows. The window displays featured electronics and musical instruments. Everything was so shiny and clean that it was hard to remember the pieces weren't new.

"Ready to meet your first pawn shop?" Ian asked as he paused with his hand on the door.

Annie just nodded and then followed him through the door. The inside surprised her as much as the street view. The store was well lit and very clean. Long showcases featured a wide variety of jewelry, including a whole shelf of lovely pocket watches. Along one wall, musical instruments of all sorts were displayed. There was even a tiny grand piano next to one front window.

Along the other wall, televisions dominated, though various kinds of electronics also were represented. There was even a glass case of notebook and tablet computers. The back wall was hung with a few paintings. As soon as she spotted them, Annie headed toward the wall. If that was the art area, that was where she was mostly likely to find Ian's sculpture.

A thin, bald man with a neat mustache stood behind the jewelry counter when they walked in, but he followed Annie toward the paintings at the back. "Are you shopping for a painting?" he asked.

"Do you get much trade in art?" Ian responded.

The man turned toward him. "No, hardly any. I took these few pieces as mercy pawn mostly. My brother is always yelling at me for that."

"Are you and your brother in this business together?" Annie asked.

The man nodded. "We thought about calling it Badler Brothers Pawn, but Joel thought that sounded too much like we were Old West outlaws."

Annie chuckled at the man's joke as she turned back to look over the paintings. There were no sculptures on display, and the fine layer of dust on the frames of the paintings suggested none of them were recently moved. "Is this all the art you have?"

"Well," the man said sheepishly. "I have a velvet portrait of Elvis, but Joel made me hide it in the back room. He said when something pulls down the atmosphere of a pawn shop, you're really in trouble."

"We're looking for one piece in particular," Ian said, pulling the photo of his sculpture from his pocket. "Has anyone come in trying to sell this?"

The man took a pair of reading glasses from his pocket and slipped them on. He peered at the photo. "No, I would remember something like that. It's really pretty."

"Could your brother have seen it?" Annie asked.

"No," the man said. "Joel's been in the hospital, and now he's in a rehab for a couple months. Car accident. So, unless this would have come in at the end of last year, he wouldn't have seen it."

"This would have been in the last few days," Ian said.

"In that case, I definitely haven't seen it."

"Could I leave my name and number?" Ian asked, handing the man a business card. "Maybe you could call me if you do get anything like this in."

The shop owner glanced down at the card. "You're the mayor of Stony Point? That's a really pretty little town."

"We like it," Ian said.

He and Annie spent a few minutes looking over the electronics, but then left. They still had a list of pawn shops to visit. The next place was also in Storm Harbor, but it was well away from Main Street. The building was brick, and the shop's only large, barred window had "Honest Bob's Gold and Pawn" painted in large letters on it.

Inside, Honest Bob's had none of the neat orderliness of the first pawn shop. Glass cases were so filled with jewelry that it looked as if the pieces were merely tossed in. The back wall had a huge neon sign reading: "Pawn, Buy, Sell!"

"Now this is more like I expected," Annie whispered.

"Welcome to Honest Bob's!" The shout came from the back of the shop where a gaunt old man stepped from a back-room door.

"Thank you," Ian said. He pointed toward the bars on the front window. "Do you get a lot of break-ins?"

The old man shook his head. "No, but we've had the front window broken out a couple of times. The police tell me that it's probably kids, but I think my neighbors just don't like pawn shops. I've never had anything stolen, but if the window is going to break that much, I figured I probably needed bars."

"I'm sorry to hear you've had so much trouble," Annie said.

"That's nice of you, ma'am. Are you and your husband looking for anything in particular?"

Before Annie could protest that Ian wasn't her husband, she was distracted by Ian's attention on one of the displays. "I see you buy art."

"Not much," the old man said. "Someone told me folk art sells really well, so I took in a few pieces last year. You can see every single one of them is still here. I suppose if folks want to buy art, they go to a gallery. Why? Are you interested in that piece? I understand it's a real nice one."

Annie walked closer to see what they were discussing. It was a carved wooden horse. Annie could see the proportions were slightly off with an oversized head and thin legs. The horse had huge teeth that it bared in a fierce grin. The wood had been painted in bright colors, and then distressed so the look was less garish, but somehow sadder. It was a strange animal and oddly compelling. "I like it," she said.

"Really?" Ian sounded surprised. He peered at the horse, as if looking for what had caught Annie's eye.

"Yes," she said. "How much do you want for it?"

The man quoted a reasonable price, and Annie accepted. As the man rung up the purchase, Ian wandered around the store, looking especially closely at the electronics. Finally he gave the man his card as he had with the previous shop owner.

When they were outside, he looked pointedly at Annie's purchase. "Did you really like that? Because you don't need to soften up the shop owners by buying things."

"No, it's OK. I really like it," Annie said. She couldn't really explain her attachment to the horse. It didn't go with her decorating tastes, but something about it just charmed her. "I certainly won't run into anything else quite like it."

"That I can believe," Ian agreed.

For the rest of the morning, they drove from shop to shop. Annie saw a pawn shop with so much neon that it looked like it belonged in Las Vegas. She saw one that specialized in taxidermy, including a wall of deer heads and a swatch of fur that the owner swore had come from Bigfoot. They visited one pawn shop tucked into an alley where the owner sat in a cage and peered out at them with distrust. In another, a huge section was filled with nothing but various tools. After each stop, Annie dashed off a text message to Alice, mostly to share the interesting things she'd seen. Alice didn't respond, and Annie hoped she was having a pleasant day with Jim.

Ian walked out of the last shop carrying a cardboard box load of purchases.

"And you teased me about buying one horse," Annie said as she followed him to the car.

"I know," he admitted sheepishly. "But I can put these tools to good use, and the prices were great."

When they reached the car, Ian proposed a stop for lunch. They found a coffee and bakeshop with candy-striped walls and a sweet antique decor. Annie was delighted to see they had something they called a "ploughman's lunch" since she wasn't really in the mood for more sweet foods. She and Ian each ordered the ploughman's lunch and coffee from the pleasant gray-haired owner.

The owner brought them a large plate of different cheeses and breads, and two smaller plates with it. "By combining, I was able to give you the best selection," she said. "Is that OK with you? I can go redo it if not."

"This looks lovely," Ian said.

Annie broke off a piece of kelly green cheese and nibbled it. The flavor was a burst of herbs in the smooth creamy cheese. "This is delicious," she said.

The woman beamed. "I'm so glad you like it. The cheeses all come from my family's cheese business. My brother is amazing at making cheese. I'm more of a baker myself."

"Sounds like a talented family," Ian said.

The woman's bright smile grew wider. "Thank you. Let me know if you want anything else at all." She headed back to busy herself behind the counter.

"I'm surprised there aren't more people in here having lunch," Annie said. "This is delicious."

"It's probably because we're closer to suppertime than lunch," Ian answered.

Annie looked at him in surprise and looked at her watch. "Time just flew today."

"We've been busy," Ian said as he tore open one of the rolls on the plate and spread it with a soft cheese. "But we only have two pawn shops left on our list."

"I just wish we'd had better luck," Annie said.

Ian nodded. "I do too. We may find a clue yet, and at least we have all these pawn shop owners on the lookout for my sculpture."

"Maybe the thief hasn't started getting rid of things yet," Annie said. "Or maybe he stole the art for himself—or herself—and the electronics to sell. If so, then it's good that Jim and Alice will be in Isabelle Murkleson's house. They may spot something."

"Do you really think she might be involved?" Ian asked.

Annie shrugged. "I don't know what to think. We don't seem to be a bit closer to solving this."

"Maybe that's why people normally leave this sort of thing to the police," Ian said. "They are trained for it."

"I would be thrilled if Chief Edwards solved this," Annie said. "I don't need credit for it. I just want the burglaries to stop. People are getting scared. Do you know Kate was afraid to take Vanessa to see Logan's play? She was afraid of being robbed while she was out of town. I hate seeing my friends hurt or scared."

Ian reached out and covered her hand with his own. "And that is one of the special things about you."

"Not so special," she said with a laugh. "I doubt anyone

likes to see friends hurt. That's pretty close to the definition of friendship."

Ian opened his mouth to reply when the shop owner walked up with a small plate. On it were two tiny chocolate cupcakes with chocolate frosting and a delicate filigree heart made from piped chocolate. "I haven't had two people so obviously in love in my shop in a while," she said. "It reminds me of my own younger days. I wanted to give you two something for brightening my day." She set the plate on the table and then hurried away before either could protest her assumptions.

"Wow, so far today we've been assumed to be married and to be in love," Annie said. "Must be something in the air."

"Must be," Ian said, smiling slightly. "But it ended in chocolate."

"That *is* a bonus," Annie said, picking up the small cupcake and taking a bite.

After lunch, Annie and Ian made quick work of the rest of the list, but struck out at both of the last shops. "Well, now I know more about pawn shops than I ever thought I would," Annie said as they walked back to Ian's car after the last shop visit.

Ian nodded, his face glum. "I hope Alice and Jim had a more productive day."

Annie agreed.

The trip back to Stony Point took a couple hours. Since both Ian and Annie were tired from the long day, conversation in the car soon dried up, and they rode in silence. The monotony of the passing scenery eventually lulled Annie to sleep. She didn't wake up until Ian's tires bit into the gravel as he pulled into the driveway in front of Grey Gables.

Annie looked around at the twilight gloom. "Oh, my," she said. "I'm sorry I fell asleep. I meant to stay awake and keep you company."

"The snoring was company enough," Ian said.

Annie looked at him in horror. "I snored?"

He laughed. "Not really. I was teasing. You do talk in your sleep though."

In a panic, Annie tried to remember what she might have been dreaming. She just drew a blank. "Did I say anything ... interesting?"

"Nothing I could understand. Just murmurs."

Annie breathed a sigh of relief. Not that she had kept any secrets from Ian, but dreams were such a private thing. "Well, thanks for an unusual day. I suppose we should get together with Alice and Jim after church tomorrow and see what they learned today."

"That sounds like a plan," Ian said. "Would you like me to walk you up?"

"Oh no, that's not necessary," Annie said, quickly swinging the car door open. "I'll be fine. And Boots is probably on a rampage again. It's better if she doesn't know you were involved in keeping me away all day."

"I have noticed that little cat can hold a grudge," Ian said.

Annie laughed. "Little? Boots is quite hefty for a cat her age. I try to keep her weight down, but she wears me down demanding food."

"I suppose I judge size by Tartan," Ian said.

"Who is probably missing you too," Annie said. "So, good night and thanks again."

Ian smiled. "Good night, Annie. I'll see you at church."

"You too." Annie hopped out of the car and hurried to the porch. She felt disappointed somehow, not so much by their fruitless pawn shop tour, as by Ian letting her walk to the porch by herself. She shook it off, scolding herself for acting like a teenager hoping for a good-night kiss.

She slipped into Grey Gables, and the loud voice of Boots brought her back to the real world again. For once, Annie appreciated that.

～ 14 ～

On Saturday morning, at the same time that Annie and Ian were driving out of Stony Point, heading for their first pawn shop, Alice tied a bright green-and-gold scarf around her auburn curls as she walked down her porch steps to head for her car. Jim caught her arm at the bottom of the stairs. "Are you all right?" he asked.

"Of course," Alice said, flashing a toothy smile. "I'm great."

"You just seem a little distant today," he said.

Her smile ached a little on her face. "Just thinking about the mystery."

Jim nodded, but his face reflected his doubt. "Well, if I did anything wrong, I hope you'll tell me. I don't read minds."

"I don't expect you to," Alice assured him. In fact, she was glad he couldn't. He'd know just how much she was starting to tie herself in knots. She was glad Jim hadn't proposed. She really was. Except when she wasn't. She knew her feelings weren't completely rational, and she intended to keep them to herself.

As Alice pulled the car out on the road, Jim tried again. "Is it this plan?" he asked. "You don't feel bad about pretending to be my assistant?"

"Of course not," Alice said. "You forget, I've actually *been* your assistant on shoots before. I enjoy it."

Jim shifted in his seat so he could watch her profile as she drove. She chose to pretend it wasn't happening. The sun felt warm on Alice's head, and the breeze through her hair was exhilarating. She was with her favorite guy on a beautiful day, and she was acting weird. She knew it. She just didn't know how to not do it.

"Did you hear from Annie this morning?" Jim asked.

"I called her while you were still sleeping," Alice said. "She's an early riser, and she left with Ian to start their sleuthing a little while ago." Then Alice smiled. "I should amend that. Annie is an early riser when she doesn't have a cold. When she has a cold, she's a human zombie."

Jim smiled. "She'd be thrilled with that description."

"But she would concede its accuracy." Annie was the least vain person Alice knew. She tended to be more comfortable with a teasing quip than with a compliment.

"I hope she has a successful time with the mayor today," Jim said.

"I hope we both find some useful clues," Alice said. "This mystery has been going nowhere fast."

"Well, that's how it works. You poke at the mystery until something pops up. It's the same when I'm trying to find the perfect spot to photograph. I just keep going until it shows up. The results are often amazing. You just have to keep looking, keep moving, and the perfect moment will come and dazzle you."

"Then you must be in a constant state of amazement."

Jim's gaze sharpened at Alice's tone. "I didn't know you had a problem with my traveling."

"I don't," Alice said. "Ignore me. I'm probably still a

little sleep deprived from the other night when we rushed to Ian's house."

"Alice, if you don't like my being gone so much, you know you can come with me. I *want* you to come with me. I do my best work when you're with me." Jim reached out to put a warm hand on her cheek. "I do my best *everything* when you're with me."

Alice patted his arm, easing his hand away. "I'm OK. Really. Like I said, just ignore me."

"Ignoring you is one thing I could never do."

Alice glanced over at Jim again and wondered just what kind of idiot she really was. Though the mood in the car was a little less tense, Jim still watched her curiously for the rest of the drive. Alice was hugely relieved when they pulled up in front of the ultramodern house that belonged to Isabelle Murkleson.

"You know, I'm surprised Stony Point let a contractor build houses like this," Jim said. "A lot of New England towns have rules about what sort of architecture they allow. They don't want to ruin the village look."

Alice nodded. "Unfortunately, this is just past the city limit. So, it uglies up Stony Point without quite breaking the rules."

They got out of the car, and Jim began looping camera bags and loose cameras over Alice's neck. Once she was well loaded, he pressed a book into her hands. "Just in case we need it."

Then he hung one smaller camera around his own. "That should impress her," he said.

"Assuming it doesn't strangle me," Alice responded.

"We all suffer so much for art."

Alice followed Jim up the narrow sidewalk to the front door. "You know this place doesn't get any better looking up close," Alice said quietly.

"Play nice," Jim told her as he pressed the doorbell.

Ms. Murkleson opened the door and scowled at Jim. "Yes?"

Jim smiled and handed her his business card. Alice glanced with interest at it. She didn't know Jim *had* business cards. The card was pretty—glossy with a close-up photo of weathered bricks for a background. "I'm Jim Parker," he said. "I'm working on a new photo book on cutting-edge architecture and design. I was driving by, and I love these houses and hope to feature one in my next book."

"You're a photographer?" the thin blonde said skeptically.

Jim nodded, and then reached back and snapped his fingers at Alice. Alice thrust the book at him, mentally making a note to discuss the snapping fingers bit later. Jim passed the book to Ms. Murkleson. "This is the book I did on lighthouses."

The woman leafed through the book. The gorgeous and artistic photos clearly impressed her. "My house would end up in a book like this?" she asked.

"It could," Jim said.

"Do you intend to include photos of the homeowners?"

"If they're willing."

Ms. Murkleson smiled. She clearly loved the idea of being photographed for a book. "Please," she said. "Come in." She turned a scornful glance toward Alice. For a moment Alice froze, hoping Ms. Murkleson wouldn't mention having seen her before at the kennel. Instead, the platinum-blond woman only said, "Be sure to have your assistant wipe her feet before she comes in. My carpets are white."

Alice grumbled inwardly as she scraped her shoes on the mat. *What kind of idiot buys white carpets?* she asked herself. *Even if you had everyone take off their shoes, you can still get food on the floor.* She watched the painfully thin woman walk ahead of them into the house. *Maybe she doesn't allow food in the house either.*

Alice looked around curiously as they walked through the house. Jim kept up a running commentary about the woman's good taste. Alice thought the place looked cold and institutional, but she knew Jim was carrying on the banter to stay in Isabelle's good graces. The color scheme was primarily black, white, and chrome. The spots of red that appeared unexpectedly reminded Alice more of a crime scene on television than of a comfortable room decor. Alice paid special attention to any artwork they passed, which was easy to spot as each piece was carefully lit—and all of them were abstracts in stark black and white that matched the rest of the rooms perfectly.

"Aren't you going to take any photos?" Ms. Murkleson asked.

"I like to get a feel for my subject before I put a lens between us," Jim said. "It helps me establish an intimacy with beauty."

Alice thought his gravelly voice was entirely too sexy to be aimed at the snobby scarecrow with overly bleached hair. Ms. Murkleson, however, clearly ate it up. Alice scowled at him. She knew it was all an act, but having him so clearly flirting with a woman half his age made her feel grumpy.

Jim managed to charm them into every room in the

house. Alice silently tromped along behind them while Isabelle pretended she wasn't there at all. The woman was clearly smitten with Jim's rakish charm despite their age difference. He even convinced her to open closets and bathrooms for his inspection. "I'm amazed at the amount of detail you've put into this decor," he said.

"I don't believe in doing anything halfway," she purred back at him.

Alice fought the urge to gag. She shifted the straps on the cameras so they didn't cut into her neck. She was beginning to think they were on a wild goose chase, and only the goose and gander were enjoying it.

"So, do you have a basement or any other storage areas?" Jim asked.

For the first time, the strangeness of his questions seemed to sink into Ms. Murkleson's head. "Why would you want to know if I had more storage?"

Jim smiled smoothly. "You have some gorgeous artwork on display, and I was wondering if you might have even more in storage. Sometimes light shining on just the right piece makes an amazing photo. I just haven't seen the perfect sculpture for that kind of solo treatment. I picture the fall of your blond hair in the background and some dark sculpture in the foreground with sunlight playing on the shape."

"Oh, that does sound good," Ms. Murkleson agreed, fluffing her hair slightly. "But I'm afraid I don't have any other storage. Just the pieces you see, and all my sculptures are white."

"That's OK," he said. "I wonder about getting a

shot of you standing in front of one of these huge windows, with a starry sky behind you to contrast with your pale beauty."

"Like a vampire?" she chirped. "I love vampire movies."

Alice stifled a groan as she shifted the heavy cameras on her shoulders again. This woman was clearly not smart enough to be a master criminal. Jim caught her impatient look, but he turned his back on her.

"So, do you live here alone, Ms. Murkleson?" he asked.

"Do call me Isabelle," she said. "No, I normally share the space with Paris, my Pomeranian."

"I hope your little dog isn't ill," Jim said.

"No, nothing like that," she said. "I just have a friend visiting who is allergic, so Paris is in the kennel."

"Oh?" Jim said with a grin. "Is your friend as beautiful as you?"

Isabelle laughed. "Well ...."

Before she could explain further, they turned at the sound of someone coming into the room. It was the man that Alice and Annie had seen on the balcony. Thankfully, he was completely dressed this time.

"Isabelle," he said, his voice disapproving, "I didn't know you were expecting company."

"I wasn't," she said. "This was a total surprise." She immediately introduced Jim—and ignored Alice—telling the man about Jim's photography.

The man stared at them incredulously. "You want to photograph these ugly houses?"

"He thinks they're impressive architecture," Isabelle said loftily.

The man narrowed his eyes as he looked at Jim. "OK, assuming that's a lie, what exactly are you doing here?"

"Just like I said," Jim answered. "I'm a photographer. I do photo books. These houses are definitely an unexpected find in New England. But I didn't get your name?"

"Livingston," the man said. "Dr. Martin Livingston. "I'm a cardiac surgeon from New York. And Isabelle is my girlfriend."

"No worries," Jim said. "I wasn't trying to cut in on your territory."

"Territory?" Isabelle snapped. "I am *not* territory."

Alice raised an eyebrow. The woman might be smarter than she thought.

"Look," Jim said. "I don't want any trouble. Maybe it would be better if we left."

"Maybe it would," Martin said.

"It does look like Martin and I need to have a talk," Isabelle said, her voice frosty. "Thank you for stopping by." She strode to a glass-and-chrome writing desk and scribbled something on the back of Jim's card. Then she handed it back to him. "Call me later, and we can set up a time for you to come back for photographs." She smiled directly into Jim's eyes. "Feel free to come alone. I don't mind carrying as many of your cameras as you need."

"Hey!" Martin said. "Exactly what's been going on here?"

"Nothing that should matter to you," Isabelle snapped.

The doctor stepped up and took a swing at Jim. Jim ducked the punch neatly and Martin's hand smacked hard into a twisted ceramic vase full of white tree branches. The vase went flying, and Isabelle began shrieking. She picked up a branch and promptly smacked Martin with it.

Jim and Alice hurriedly left before the doctor decided to take another swing at Jim. Just as they reached the car, Alice started giggling. "You were asking for that."

"Me?" Jim said as he pulled open the car door. "I was perfectly polite."

"You were flirting with that woman outrageously the whole time we were there. She looked ready to eat you up."

"Hey, it gave us a chance to search the place. Did you see any of the missing artwork?"

"Well, judging from the stark difference between the Dunhams' decorating taste and Isabelle Murkleson's—I'm certain none of the paintings in there were the stolen one. And I definitely didn't see Ian's dancer statuette either. Plus, that woman didn't seem bright enough to be a successful burglar."

"Her boyfriend is smart though." Jim slipped into the car. "But I can't say that I think they're the crooks either."

Alice slipped the key in the ignition and then said, "I should check my messages before we take off, in case Annie called." She pulled out her cellphone and found the string of texts from Annie. Read all at once, they formed an almost running commentary on each pawn shop. One post made Alice laugh out loud.

"Not fair," Jim complained. "You have to share. Did she and the mayor find anything yet?"

"They found a piece of Bigfoot pelt," Alice said. "And Annie says she bought a great grinning horse sculpture. Otherwise, no; the mystery tour of pawn shops hasn't been very successful yet."

"The Bigfoot pelt *is* interesting," Jim said. "Do you know

if it was supposed to come from around here? I didn't know they had any Bigfoot legends in New England."

Alice glanced at him from the corner of her eye. "I expect it was bear fur or beaver, maybe. And I've never heard any local Bigfoot stories."

"Bigfoot stories do pop up in the strangest places," Jim said. "I heard some interesting stories about the skunk ape when we were down tracking the demon dogs in South Carolina. I would do a book on monsters, but the photo opportunities are a little slim."

"That would probably come from the monsters being imaginary," Alice said.

"Maybe," Jim agreed. "But you never know. The world is full of strange things."

"I agree," Alice said. "You don't know how strange it was to watch you flirting with someone who could have been your daughter."

"Hey, I was taking one for the team," he protested. "You know I only have eyes for you, Red."

Alice dropped the phone back into her purse and started the car. "I think when we get back to my house, we should see if we can find any information about a surgeon named Martin Livingston—preferably with a photo so we can be sure this guy isn't borrowing someone else's name."

"He could be," Jim said. "He looked weaselly."

"Based on what? How quickly he saw through our little charade?" Alice asked. "Or how much he didn't like you flirting with his girlfriend?"

"What?" Jim asked. "You're crankier with me now than

before. You can't really be jealous of Isabelle Murkleson. I like my ladies with a little more upstairs."

"I don't know," Alice said. "She kept thrusting what she had upstairs into your face whenever she could."

"Alice," Jim said. "I meant higher upstairs." Jim tapped his temple. "And you know it. I don't like you being mad at me, but this new jealous thing is kind of cute. I didn't know you had it in you."

"I don't know what you're talking about," she grumbled.

"Sure you don't," he said. "You know, my laptop is in my bag, and they have free Wi-Fi at the diner. We're closer to Main Street than to your house. What say we have some lunch and check out the doctor at the same time? Maybe a little hot food will cheer you up."

Alice glanced at him. "I'm not really hungry."

"I promise not to flirt with Peggy," he coaxed.

"Peggy is not interested in you. Isabelle Murkleson was."

"It's my raw animal charm," he said with a grin.

Alice snorted.

Jim put his hand over his heart in mock pain. "You used to like my raw animal charm."

"I used to like Scooby-Doo cartoons too," Alice said. "Sometimes things change."

"What?" Jim said, his voice full of shock. "You don't like Scooby-Doo cartoons? Are you even an American?"

"OK, but I only like the old ones," Alice admitted.

"I agree," Jim said. "When they brought in Scrappy-Doo, the show became a complete artistic failure. Plus, I missed the redhead."

Alice couldn't help laughing. "You would."

They continued to banter for the rest of the drive to The Cup & Saucer, and it lightened the mood between them. Jim stopped asking what was bothering her. After they reached the diner, Peggy settled them at a table with her usual cheerful efficiency. Alice pulled out her phone and asked, "Do you think I should send Annie an update on our lack of progress?"

"Maybe you should save it until we can get together to plan our next move," Jim said as he pulled a laptop computer out of his camera bag and brought up an Internet search engine. It only took a few moments to find a photo of the doctor.

"Well, another suspect bites the dust," Alice said.

"The day wasn't a total loss, you know," Jim said. "Eliminating a suspect is a kind of progress."

"Then we've done great so far," Alice answered. "We know the burglar isn't the kennel owners, the guy who works there, or the suspicious purse-dog owner. We're rapidly working ourselves down to no suspects."

"Maybe we need to run at this from a new angle," Jim said. "What names have popped up related to this case that you didn't ever consider a suspect?"

"Well, the Freemans' niece works at the kennel during the summer," Alice said. "She's going to college in the fall for veterinary medicine. She seemed like a really nice girl, and she's clearly very fond of her aunt and uncle."

"And since she's nice, she can't be a crook," Jim said.

"Something like that."

"Because the nice person has never had dangerous secrets in any of the mysteries you and Annie have tackled in the past," Jim said.

Alice sighed. "Yes, sometimes we've misjudged people. And sometimes nice people have done bad things. We should probably ask a few more questions about the niece."

Jim pulled a notebook from his pocket and began making a list. "Who else has popped up without being suspects?"

"The victims, of course," Alice said. "After all, they were robbed. But why would anyone steal their own stuff? Plus, they were all out of town at the time of their own robbery."

"Or so they *say*." Jim shrugged. "As for motive, that's easy: for insurance or to be sure not to be considered a suspect."

"OK, so we should check out the victims," Alice agreed. "So, are you ready to grill Ian to be sure he's not the burglar?"

Jim laughed. "No, I think we'll leave that stone unturned."

"The only other person who has come up is the crabby neighbor," Alice said.

"Whose crabby neighbor?"

"The one next door to the Freemans," Alice answered. "They said their neighbor complained a lot about the kennel—so much so that they had to get additional soundproofing. But that's it. We didn't have any reason to consider him a suspect."

"We should still look at him," Jim said. "When the obvious suspects don't pan out, you have to start looking at the unlikely ones."

"Right. So that means you should grill Ian."

"What?" Jim said. "Are you sad that the doctor didn't manage to punch me, so you want Ian to give it a try?"

"Ian's not the violent sort."

"Maybe not normally, but I don't always bring out the best in the guy."

Alice grinned. "Must be your raw animal charm."

Jim laughed aloud at that just as Peggy arrived with their lunch. Jim tucked his list into his pocket. "Let's call an end to sleuthing for the day," he said. "I want to just spend some quality time with my lady on such a beautiful day."

Alice pushed a smile onto her face. "Sounds good to me."

~ 12 ~

Sunday dawned with the kind of bright, breezy beauty that only Maine can offer. Annie picked a sundress in a pale floral and topped it with a cotton short-sleeve cardigan. The combination felt delicate and feminine, perfect for a sunny summer day. She ran a brush through her fine, straight hair and chose a delicate floral barrette to pin it up on one side.

Annie was happy to go to church and listen to Reverend Wallace talk about something besides the break-ins. She was feeling a little depressed about their lack of success in tracking down the culprit, even though she knew it was much more a job for the police than for her. She'd enjoyed every moment of spending Saturday with Ian, but they'd gotten no closer to finding Ian's sculpture.

As she stood next to Ian, sharing a hymnbook and singing, she pushed away the nagging feeling of guilt about having failed him—she'd failed to keep his house from being robbed, and failed to unearth anything to bring back his late wife's sculpture.

She knew Ian didn't blame her. He didn't need to. She generated enough guilt all on her own.

When the songs were sung and the congregation settled into the pews, Reverend Wallace stepped up to the pulpit and smiled across the congregation. "When I look at you this morning, I see a congregation of believers, but I see more than that. I see a community, a strong community, a community with heart. I see people who are quick to help one another in the rough times, people who are quick to bring comfort in tragedy and quick to share laughter in times of joy. The strength of a church isn't in the number of bodies in the seats, but the level of community in the people's hearts."

Annie relaxed while the Reverend's warm voice washed over her as he expanded his sermon to talk about always being an open community—welcoming the newcomer, lending a hand to the neighbors beyond the town limits, taking part in the larger community of Maine. Annie loved the community she'd adopted—and which had adopted her—after the death of her grandmother. She knew her curiosity and tendency to be stubborn drove much of her mystery solving, but community drove the rest. She wanted to help and give something back to these people. Like Reverend Wallace, she believed the people of Stony Point were special and blessed.

Of course, she knew equally well that neither her friends nor she were perfect. Her eyes swept the congregation quietly. Stella Brickson was one of her dear friends now, but the woman had given her full attention to freezing Annie out when she first came to Stony Point. Mary Beth felt like a big sister now, but an old family secret of hers had nearly gotten Annie killed. And sweet, gentle Kate had once believed Annie capable of chasing after her ex-husband in the middle of another mystery that had also almost gotten Annie killed. As Annie thought about the last few years since she had moved to Stony Point, it was no wonder Ian worried about her safety so much!

Annie's attention drifted between the congregation and the pulpit for the rest of the service. She knew her edginess was a normal side effect of being so caught up in the new mystery, but she still let it add to her present guilt. She'd felt like a fidgety child during church and knew that wasn't the best response to the beautiful service.

Afterward, Annie smiled and greeted the people standing around her. Her eyes met Alice, waving near the sanctuary doors. Jim stood beside her, looking mildly uncomfortable in a crisply ironed shirt. Alice gestured to meet outside, and Annie nodded.

Ian and Annie moved slowly toward the door. As mayor of Stony Point, Ian was well known by everyone, and it seemed they all had something brief to say to him. Some offered their condolences on his recent break-in. Others were clearly afraid and asked what he was going to do to make the town safer. "I feel like I'm trapped in town," one elderly woman said. "It seems that every time someone goes on a trip, they come home to find their home robbed. I was going to visit my sister. She's ill and could use my help, but I don't dare leave my house alone."

"Chief Edwards is working hard on the case," Ian assured her. The woman's huff made it clear how impressed she was with the chief's efforts.

"Well, at least tell me if it's true that everyone robbed used that kennel at the edge of town," the woman demanded. "I don't want to put my poor Poopsie in a place run by thieves."

"I'm sure no one believes the kennel owners are thieves," Annie said.

Another huff. "That's not what I've heard!"

Finally Annie and Ian made it to the front steps of the church. "Whew," Annie whispered. "I didn't realize people were so worried, though I don't like to see them blame you, and I'm not happy to hear they're blaming the kennel. I'm certain the owners are not thieves."

"They need a place to unload some of their worry," Ian said lightly. "Once Chief Edwards finds the real culprits, all the speculation will be over. I suspect he has a much harder time than us. If people are blaming me, imagine how they're responding to him."

Annie nodded. She was sure the chief was finding it a tough time to be the head of the police department.

She looked around the parking lot for Alice and Jim. Instead, she caught sight of Chief Edwards himself. He'd made it nearly to the parking lot before being surrounded by distressed community members whose agitated gestures made Annie glad she wasn't in the middle of them. "Looks like you were right," she said, drawing Ian's attention to the group.

"I wonder if I should try to rescue him," Ian said.

"We could try," Annie suggested.

"Mrs. Dawson! Mayor Butler!"

Annie and Ian turned to find Vanessa running out of the church.

"Is everything OK?" Annie asked.

Vanessa nodded, gasping. "Sorry, I was in the toddler nursery and couldn't leave until everyone picked up their children. I was afraid I might miss you." She handed a small stack of papers to Ian. "I spent all day yesterday looking at auction sites, but I couldn't find anything," she said, her voice still a little wheezy. "Then last night, I put a post up on this networking site I hang out on. I asked if anyone knew about other art auction sites. Someone did! And I checked this morning before church. I found your sculpture!" She tapped the pile of paper. "I printed out all the information on it. The auction just started this morning."

Ian carefully unfolded the papers. The auction had a clear photo of the sculpture, and there was no doubt—it was the little dancer. "This is fantastic, Vanessa," he said. "You might have solved this case."

Vanessa glowed. "I thought you'd be excited."

"And I am. If you'll excuse me, I need to take this to Chief Edwards." Ian turned immediately and hurried down the church steps, nearly sprinting to the group where Chief Edwards struggled to placate everyone.

Annie gave Vanessa a hug. "Thank you so much for spending all the time to do this. We were feeling a little down after a day of very fruitless sleuthing."

Vanessa blushed. "It wasn't a big deal. I could tell Mayor Butler was really sad about the sculpture. I wanted to help." Vanessa glanced across the churchyard where she could see Chief Edwards gesturing at the group to give him and Ian some space. Though some people moved along, several lurked as close as they could. "Do you think we could go over and see what the chief is going to do now? I don't want to get in trouble, but I guess I am kind of curious. I'd love to know how they track down people from the auction."

Annie grinned. "Me too. Of course, trying to satisfy my curiosity is normally how I get into trouble."

Since Annie and Vanessa couldn't move as quickly in their dress shoes, Ian and Chief Edwards were mostly finished by the time they arrived. The Chief merely greeted them politely before hurrying off to his car. The small crowd around him parted, and Annie could see that those who had remained to eavesdrop mostly looked much more cheerful. Seeing such a great clue arrive had clearly given them all hope. The crowd broke up, drifting away in small groups to talk about the latest development.

"I couldn't exactly pass on the auction information in secret," Ian to Annie and Vanessa. "But I passed it on."

"I think it actually helped people to see something happening," Annie assured him.

"What's the chief going to do?" Vanessa asked.

"Track down whoever is running that auction," Ian said. "And hopefully arrest the thief and return everyone's things. I was sure to tell him that it was you who tracked down the auction information, Vanessa."

Vanessa smiled again. "Well, I'd better go find my mom. Will you let me know what happens with the auction?"

"I will," Ian promised.

As Vanessa hurried away, Annie was suddenly struck by a thought and began looking around the parking lot. "You know, Alice waved us outside. I was expecting to find them out here."

"Maybe they got tired of waiting," Ian said. "I wasn't able to get out of the church very quickly."

"Maybe," Annie said, though it wasn't like Alice to be

impatient with her. She fished around in her purse until she found her cellphone. When she turned it on, she found a message from Alice. She and Jim were having brunch at Maplehurst Inn and would be at Annie's house in the late afternoon for a mystery meeting.

"That's weird," Annie said. "They didn't even invite us to join them for lunch. I thought she'd want to catch up after yesterday."

"Maybe Jim wanted a more intimate lunch," Ian said. "We men sometimes forget how much women need to connect with one another."

"Oh, because men never do that," Annie said.

"Not quite the same way," Ian said. "But I do think they had a great idea about having a nice lunch. Where would you like me to take you?"

"That is a lovely offer, Mr. Mayor," Annie said, "but I need to get home so I can straighten up and make some snacks for our mystery meeting."

"But you said Alice and Jim were having lunch right now," Ian said. "Why would they want snacks?"

"It's not about whether they're hungry," Annie explained patiently. "It's about being a good hostess."

Ian opened his mouth to say something else and then closed it again. "OK. Do you want me to come with you and help?"

Annie shook her head. "No, thank you. Maybe you could go take Tartan for a walk. It'll help pass the time until you hear from the chief. Do you think he'll track down the thief today?"

"That would be a nice thought, wouldn't it, though he

may simply try to buy into the auction and catch the thief by tracking him down afterward," Ian said. He reached out and gave Annie's hand a squeeze. "Well, since I'm clearly being dismissed, I'll see you later this afternoon."

"Oh, not dismissed," Annie said. "I just need to clean up and ...."

"I understand. I think." Ian lifted a strand of hair away from Annie's face. "Don't work too hard."

"I won't," Annie assured him.

He turned and walked toward his car. She watched his long-legged stride and thought how much it mirrored a picture of Ian's nature. He didn't vacillate. He decided on a course of action and went after it. Annie decided she could use more of that herself.

With a self-deprecating sigh, she headed for her own car and began planning her snack menu as she headed for home. Since she'd cleaned house so recently, she really only needed to do a little light dusting. After some bribe kibble to keep Boots from yowling at her, Annie toasted some thin slices of Italian bread for crostini to go with some mild cheese Alice had brought her from the farmers market. Then she began whipping up some stuffing for cherry tomatoes. As she worked, she hummed tunelessly. Each time worrisome thoughts about the mystery tried to intrude, Annie just hummed louder.

Finally, she stopped, nearly giggling, as a memory came to mind. The last time she'd been back in Texas to visit, she'd walked in on an argument between Joanna and John. John was shouting at his sister as she stood with her fingers in her ears humming loudly between shouts of "I can't hear you." Annie felt the same way as she chased her guilty thoughts out of her head.

She returned to her food preparation and intentionally filled her head with happy snippets of memory about the twins. Though they sometimes drove their mom crazy, even their squabbles made Annie laugh. The two children were such perfect opposites in so many ways. As a result, they were perfect friends and passionate enemies several times every day.

Annie wondered what it would have been like to have a sibling. Like her daughter, Annie had been an only child, though Annie and Alice were so close as children they sometimes felt more than a little like sisters. They could drive each other crazy back then.

Smiling, Annie began arranging her finished snacks on trays. She hoped John and Joanna would grow up to be strong, sure friends, just as she and Alice had. Annie quickly covered the trays to prevent a feline snack attack. She had just finished when she heard the doorbell.

She walked through the hall, wiping her hands on a kitchen towel. She was surprised to see Ian at the door. She'd expected Alice and Jim as she'd seen them pull in next door over a half an hour earlier. Since they only had to walk across the lawn, Annie was surprised that they hadn't arrived first.

"Am I too early?" Ian asked as he stepped through the door.

"No," Annie said, giving him a quick hug and a kiss. "You're just perfect. I finished all my chores."

Boots rushed into the hallway and gave Ian's pants a

sniff before backing away with a glare. "Ah," Annie said. "I see you spent some quality time with Tartan."

"I wish Boots was a little more open to the idea of making friends with Tartan," Ian said ruefully. "I wonder if it would help if they spent some time together."

"I'm not sure it would help Tartan much," Annie said. "He'd probably end up with a dire cat phobia."

"Boots does seem rather set in her ways," Ian said.

Ian followed Annie into the living room and settled on the sofa. "Did you hear from the chief?" Annie asked.

Ian sighed and nodded. "He wasn't able to track the auction back to the owner. Apparently this thief is very good at covering his computer tracks. The auction has been withdrawn, though, with no sale. The chief wasn't sure why. He made one bid and the auction ended. But at least the little dancer didn't end up sold to someone else. If we catch the thief, we should be able to recover the sculpture."

"Oh, Ian," Annie said. "I'm so sorry. That was our best lead. I really hoped it would turn up a name."

Ian settled back against the sofa, stretching his long legs out in front of him. "I haven't given up hope. The chief is a very competent man."

Annie jumped as the doorbell rang again. "That must be Alice and Jim."

Ian stood, but didn't follow Annie out into the hallway. She greeted the couple at the door. "Ian beat you this time," Annie told them.

"I wanted to change out of my church clothes," Alice said, her voice slightly strained. "I thought that would be all right."

"Of course it's all right," Annie said. "I didn't mean to sound critical."

"You didn't," Jim said warmly. "Alice is being a grouch today—as she was yesterday."

Alice frowned at him, but didn't say anything, so Jim looked around the hall. "I notice I haven't been threatened by your cat yet. She's not sick, I hope."

"No, she's not sick," Annie said as she led them into the living room. "She's sulking because she could smell Ian's dog on his pants."

"Ah, dueling pets," Jim said. "At least Alice and I don't have to deal with that."

"Pets would be too much commitment," Alice said, giving Jim a fierce look. Jim just stared back, looking confused at first and then resigned.

"Alice, could you help me bring in the snacks?" Annie asked.

"Of course."

Alice followed Annie into the kitchen. "Oh, these look yummy," Alice said as she looked over the trays.

"I hope so," Annie said. "Alice, are you OK? You seem a little out of sorts. Is something going on between you and Jim?"

Alice smiled. "I'm probably just a little tired. We better get these back to the living room. You know it's not a good idea to leave Jim and Ian alone."

"I'm sure they're fine," Annie said. "If you want to talk about anything, I'm sure they'll wait."

"Nope," Alice said as she picked up a grape from one tray and popped it into her mouth. "I'm fine." She scooped up the tray and headed out of the kitchen, so Annie had no choice but to follow her. Something was definitely up with Alice, but Annie couldn't *make* her friend tell her what was wrong.

Annie and Alice set their trays on the coffee table. Annie caught sight of Boots sniffing the air and padding into the room. "I better shut Boots into a different room before she goes after the food." She scooped up the chubby cat and carried her upstairs to her bedroom. Annie rubbed the cat's ears as she walked and Boots responded with a rumbly purr. "Ah, if you knew what I was about to do, you wouldn't be purring at me."

Boots rubbed her head against Annie's hand for more ear massage. When they reached the bedroom, Annie settled the cat on the bed. Boots blinked sleepily at her, and Annie quickly left, shutting the door behind her.

She could hear her friends talking as she walked back into the living room. "So, we aren't really any closer to finding an answer," Alice said.

"But if we keep finding out who is *not* the burglar, eventually the only one left will be the culprit," Jim added.

"That could take a while," Ian said. "Stony Point isn't heavily populated, but with the summer swell, it could take a while to clear a few thousand people."

"That doesn't sound like the most efficient way to solve the mystery," Alice said. "I think we need to be a little more proactive."

"How's that?" Annie asked.

"I think we need to set a trap."

"Didn't we try something like that?" Jim asked. "When we staked out the Murkleson woman."

"I'm thinking more of an undercover sting," Alice said.

"You want to go undercover?" Annie asked. "As what?"

"I don't think any of us would work," Alice said. "I was thinking of a bit furrier undercover agent."

"Furrier?" Annie echoed; then realization dawned on her. "You want Boots to go undercover at the kennel *for real*?"

Jim grinned. "Knowing that creature, don't you think this is a recipe for *cat*astrophe?"

~ 13 ~

*E*veryone groaned at Jim's questionable pun. Annie looked around at her friends and saw all eyes were on her. Obviously, it was up to her whether Boots would be used to bait the trap. Annie just wasn't certain she was up for how much snubbing she would get in the aftermath.

"If it were an option," Ian said, "we'd use Tartan, but I can't really picture the thief going after my place again."

"Still, the break-ins have generally been tied to more upscale homes," Annie said.

"Grey Gables looks great these days," Alice responded. "You've put so much work into this place. The burglar probably doesn't know you. He doesn't know you live modestly. He'll just see this big house, with clear signs of recent investment in upkeep, and salivate."

Jim grinned. "You could always park the mayor's sleek little car outside. It'll help make you look upscale. Then make a big deal out of going away for a while."

"Well, I don't mind trying," Annie said. "I'd try anything that would help catch this guy. So, I'll put Boots in the kennel tomorrow and then pretend to leave. Then what? I slink around the house in the dark and wait for the burglar?"

"Not alone you don't," Ian said. "We'll wait with you."

"All of us together?" Alice asked. "You don't think that'll

be a little hard to disguise? Or do you picture us all sitting on the floor in here in the dark?"

"I dunno," Jim said. "Huddling in the dark with two beautiful ladies sounds like fun to me."

Alice rolled her eyes. "It sounds silly."

Annie looked at her friend worriedly. The words Alice said weren't that bad, but her tone wasn't normal at all. She was mad at Jim, for sure. Annie wondered if she might be mad at all of them. What could they possibly have done?

"I don't think it's a good idea for us all to wait here," Ian said. "I think we should have someone watching the kennel. If someone is breaking into the kennel at night to find out what homes are empty, then we might be able to catch the crook at that point."

"That sounds like a good idea," Alice said. "Maybe you and Jim could watch the kennel. Annie and I will stay here."

Ian and Jim turned identical shocked looks toward Alice. Ian shook his head. "I don't think that's a good idea."

"You think the good mayor could keep his mind on the stakeout knowing you and Alice are here unprotected?" Jim asked. "Plus, if I get a vote, I'd rather huddle in the dark with you, even if you are as prickly as a cactus today."

"It's one burglar, not a street gang," Alice said. "And we'd have the police on speed dial. I think Annie and I would be perfectly safe. It's not like we'd be tackling the guy in the dark. We'd just call the police if we saw him."

"No way," Ian said. "Forget it. I'll stay here with Annie."

"I don't suppose anyone would like to hear my input?" Annie asked.

Ian turned to her. His jaw was rigid with tension. She'd

seen the look before. He got it every time he felt Annie was putting herself in danger. She was touched that Ian cared so much, but she suspected that the caring could turn to controlling if she wasn't careful. "Annie," Ian said. "You know I'm not leaving you alone here if we're expecting a criminal to break in."

"Hey," Alice said. "So being here with me counts as alone? You know, Annie and I have gotten through more than one tough situation just fine."

Ian held up his hand. "OK, not alone. But definitely unprotected."

"I swing a pretty mean flashlight," Alice snapped back.

"I agree with Ian," Annie said, keeping her voice very even. "We should divide into two groups so both the house and the kennel are covered. Ian and I should stay here. Jim and Alice should watch the kennel. I don't quite know why we'd do it any other way." She turned to Alice. "Unless you and Jim would like to watch for the burglar here? Ian and I could watch the kennel."

"Fine," Alice snapped. "Whatever the group wants."

Jim stared at Alice, completely lost.

"Look, I think we need a little break from the crime talk," Annie said, hopping up from the sofa. She walked around collecting snack plates and cups. "I'll get everyone some fresh coffee. Alice, do you want to help?"

"Sure," Alice said. She stood and picked up the mostly empty snack trays and hurried from the room.

Annie reached across Ian to get his mug and whispered in his ear, "Ask Jim what's going on."

She stood with her hands full and headed across the

room. At the doorway, she glanced back at Ian, and he nodded. Then she followed Alice back down the hall to the kitchen. When she walked into the kitchen, Alice was combining the remaining snacks on a small tray. "What is going on with you tonight?" Annie asked.

"What are you talking about?" Alice asked.

Annie stared at her friend. "Ian and Jim staking out the kennel together? Really? The two of them, together? You might want to see a fight, but I don't. You know Jim and Ian get along like fire and lighter fluid."

Alice shrugged, dropping her eyes to the tray. "I thought it might be a good way for them to get to know each other and stop being so competitive. Without either of us around, they could find they have a lot in common."

Annie leaned against the counter. "It's not that I don't think that's a good idea, in theory. But the timing is suspicious. You're clearly upset with Jim for something—or else you're upset with all of us. Alice, you're my friend. Please, tell me what's going on."

"You *are* my friend, Annie," Alice said as she turned away to run water into the coffee mugs. "And if anything is going on with me, I'd be sure to tell you. Now, aren't we supposed to be getting coffee?"

Annie gave up. One thing she and Alice had in common was stubbornness. If Alice didn't want to talk about what was bothering her, she wouldn't. Annie just hoped Ian had found out something from Jim. She hated to see Alice upset.

When they returned to the living room, Annie said, "So, I'll be taking Boots to the kennel in the morning. Do you think I should go alone?"

"No," Ian said, frowning. "I'll go with you."

"I'm not sure that's a good idea," Jim said, wincing as Ian turned to glare at him. "Look, it's just that your house was just robbed. It might be better if the crook didn't associate you with Annie. We want Annie's house to look like a tempting target, remember?"

"You think the burglar keeps tabs on the kennel all day long?" Alice asked, her tone making it clear that she thought that idea was silly.

"At this point, we really don't know what the guy is doing," Jim said. "And I don't think we should take any risks."

"Risk is what I'm concerned about," Ian snapped. "Annie is not going over there alone. Not even in broad daylight."

Annie looked sharply at Ian. "Actually, I am. We want the burglar to see me as an easy mark. It's going to be daytime, and I'm just dropping off a cat. The greatest danger will be when I try to shove Boots into the cat carrier. I appreciate your concern, Ian, but this isn't dangerous."

Ian's jaw tightened, but finally he nodded. "Fine. Just call me as soon as you're done at the kennel. Would you be comfortable with that?"

Annie smiled. "I would."

"So, do we start watching the kennel as soon as Boots arrives, or wait until after hours?" Alice asked.

"The picked locks suggest the crook checks out names after hours," Ian said. "It would be difficult for him to pass unnoticed during a busy day at the kennel. You can probably wait until dark."

Jim rose stiffly from his chair. "That sounds like a plan then—one I think we should all sleep on."

"Good idea," Ian said.

Alice looked like she might object, but then Annie spoke up, "I really should be releasing Boots so she can start to forgive me for closing her up in my bedroom this evening. That way she can be freshly mad at me tomorrow when I take her to the kennel."

Jim chuckled. "Good luck with that." He turned to put his arm around Alice, but she neatly sidestepped him and headed for the door. Annie could hear Jim's sigh from across the room.

"If anything interesting happens when you drop off Boots," Alice said, "be sure to call me."

"I will," Annie agreed.

As soon as she'd bid Alice and Jim good night and had closed the door on them, she turned quickly to Ian. "Did Jim tell you what's bothering Alice?"

"He doesn't have a clue," Ian said. "Unless you count the normal observation that all women act crazy once in a while."

"Really? That doesn't make sense."

Ian smiled. "I'm afraid this is one time I side with Jim. Women are a mystery. It's actually more surprising when we *do* understand them than when we don't."

"I meant that it didn't make sense for Jim to have no idea what's bothering Alice." Annie frowned at him. "You make women sound irrational, and we're not."

"Not a bit," Ian said, leaning over to kiss Annie. "I would never, ever say that women are irrational. At least not all the time. But you *can* be challenging. Now, I should head home and get some sleep. We might have some late nights ahead of us, waiting for the burglar to strike again."

Annie nodded. She could see nothing good coming from any more discussion of whether it was men or women who behaved the most erratically. She just hoped she could sleep.

After Ian left, and Boots was given a ridiculous amount of petting to overcome the trauma of being shut up in Annie's bedroom, Annie found herself yawning. She slipped into bed, expecting to lie awake, but sleep found her quickly.

Her dreams weren't completely restful. She was back at the kennel, racing down endless hallways, looking for Boots. Somehow she was certain the burglar was going to do some harm to the cat. Annie called out to Boots again and again. Each time, she heard a yowling call of alarm, but no matter how hard she looked, she saw only fleeting shadows and blank walls.

Annie woke with a start and found Boots slapping at her face with her paw. "What are you doing?" she asked the cat.

Boots responded by snuggling against Annie and closing her eyes. Annie remembered the dream and wondered if her calling for Boots in the dream had translated into talking in her sleep. She'd imagine the cat would find it confusing to hear Annie call her over and over in the darkness.

"Well, thanks for the wake-up," she told the cat. "I wasn't enjoying that dream much." Annie stroked the cat's soft fur. She glanced over at the clock and saw it was barely past midnight. She settled down and fell back to sleep to the soft sound of the cat's purrs. If she had any more disturbing dreams, she didn't remember them.

The next morning proved to be another beautiful summer day. Annie fed Boots a good breakfast and even sneaked her some totally forbidden bacon scraps. "Guilt treats," Annie said.

Finally, it came time to put Boots in the cat carrier. Annie tossed in some bacon and Boots walked right in. When Annie closed the door of the carrier, Boots offered one offended meow, but then settled down to chewing up the bacon bribe. "Maybe this won't be that bad," Annie said as she hauled the carrier down the hallway, staggering a bit under the weight. "You know, I don't think you've lost much weight. No more bacon."

Boots rustled in the carrier but didn't bother with a vocal response. Annie buckled the carrier into the back-seat of her Malibu and then headed for the kennel. "This is going to be for a good cause," Annie said. "Try not to hate me for too long."

When she pulled up in front of the Stony Point Kennel, Annie glanced at her watch and groaned. Her nerves had made her drive a bit faster than usual, and it wasn't quite time for the kennel to open. Boots yowled, ready to be out of the carrier now that the car had stopped.

"Fine," Annie said. "Maybe they'll let me in early."

Annie walked to the front door and turned the knob, but the door was locked. She decided to walk around to the back of the kennel. She might run into someone outside prepping the outdoor runs for the day.

She was pleased to see Jensen filling water bowls at the outdoor faucet. "Mrs. Dawson," he said cheerfully. "I'm glad to see you. Thanks so much for helping with my allergy medicine. I feel a lot better."

"I'm glad," Annie said. "I've come to check Boots into the kennel, but I got here a little too early."

"No problem," he said. "I'll let you in. You'll be glad to

know that we've added a new safety measure around here. Mr. Freeman changed all the locks and added two deadbolts with no outside keyhole. They'll only use those last deadbolts at night after the kennel closes, but we can be sure no one could pick the lock and get in now."

"Oh, that's a good idea," Annie said. "But what will you do if everyone gets locked out again?"

Jensen laughed. "Pick the front lock, I guess."

"So you're still not secure."

"I think we're pretty covered at night," he said. "There are motion sensors all over the front yard. They turn on lights, and the one right at the door even sets off a buzzer upstairs. They had motion sensors and lights in the backyard for a while, but all the food bowls and water out here draw too many wild animals. The lights flicking on all night irritated the neighbor."

"I thought everything irritated the neighbor," Annie said.

"Just about."

Annie followed Jensen to the back door, which flew open just as they reached it. Marcie Freeman rushed out; her face flooded with relief when she saw Jensen. "Please, come and help me," she said.

"What's wrong?" Jensen asked, hurrying in the door after Marcie. He caught the door before it could swing shut and held it for Annie.

"It's Mr. Norman," Marcie said. She looked at Annie and whispered, "The neighbor. He stormed in as soon as I unlocked the front door. I can't seem to calm him down, and my aunt and uncle are at the store picking up supplies."

"So you think I can calm the old grouch down?" Jensen asked with grin.

"Not so much," she said. "I just feel safer with numbers."

As they walked into the front foyer, Annie spotted a man leaning over the desk, peering at something. He straightened quickly as soon as he heard them. Something about the man looked familiar. "So, I see customers are more important than the people who were here in this neighborhood long before you brought those noisy dogs here!"

"Your complaints are important too," Marcie said.

"Well, I'm tired of all the barking during the day," the man said. "I work at home, and I need to concentrate!"

"How interesting," Annie said cheerfully. "What kind of work do you do at home?"

"Who are you?" he demanded.

"Oh, I'm sorry," Marcie said. "This is Mrs. Dawson. And this is the kennel's neighbor, Mr. Norman."

"I'm pleased to meet you, Mr. Norman," Annie said pleasantly. He ignored her and turned to Marcie again. "So what are you going to do about the barking?"

"I'll tell my aunt and uncle that you stopped by," Marcie said. "And about your issue. I'm sure they'll do what they can."

He took a step closer to Marcie and raised his voice, "That's not enough!"

Jensen stepped between the man and Marcie. "I'm afraid it will have to be enough for now."

"Who do you think you are?" Mr. Norman roared.

"Mr. Norman!" Annie snapped, pulling her cellphone out of her pocket. "If you continue to behave badly, I'm going to dial the police. I came here to check my cat in to this nice kennel so I can leave town for a few days, and your behavior is preventing me from doing that."

Mr. Norman looked at Annie in shock. She was a little surprised at herself, but she hated seeing the man bully the two young people. She'd always hated bullies.

"Who did you say you are?" he growled.

"Annie Dawson," she said. "I'm Elizabeth Holden's granddaughter. And I have the police on speed dial. Do I need to make that call?"

"No," he grumbled. "I'll come back when the owners are here." He smirked at Annie. "You have a real nice trip, Mrs. Dawson." He turned and stomped out the front door.

"I wonder what got him all worked up again," Marcie said. "My aunt and uncle will be so disappointed. They were hoping he was done complaining for good."

Annie turned toward the front desk. "What was Mr. Norman looking at when we came in?"

"I don't know," Marcie said. "There's nothing interesting there. Just the check-in log and an article I'm reading on diagnosing infections through fecal examination."

Jensen snorted. "Probably the article on poop, since I'm pretty such Mr. Norman is full of—"

"Jensen!" Marcie said, her eyes cutting toward Annie. "We have a client. Now, I'm so sorry to have kept you and your kitty waiting. Let's get you checked in."

Annie patiently answered the young woman's questions, but thoughts of the mystery kept running through her mind. Why was Mr. Norman suddenly back to complaining? And why did the man's angry face look so familiar? Could it have something to do with the new locks on the back door? Was complaining the only way he could get access to the check-in log?

"Do you have a lot of pets in the kennel right now?" Annie asked when the forms were all filled out.

Marcie shook her head. "We're practically empty. Everyone is scared to go out of town. We still have poor little Paris, and thankfully, there's one other dog, since Paris gets lonely."

"Another dog?" Annie said.

"Buster," Jensen said with a laugh. "He's a French bull-dog. He belongs to these two guys who live on a boat. They took the boat down to North Carolina to party, and appar-ently Buster gets seasick on the open ocean."

"Oh, poor thing," Annie said. "But surely Boots will have company in the cat room?"

"I'm afraid not," Marcie said. "But we'll have lots of spare time, so I promise to make sure Boots is pampered to the max."

"She won't want to come home," Annie said. She thanked the two young people and handed over the cat carrier. Boots offered one disgruntled meow during the hand-off, but Annie was surprised at how calm the cat stayed. If Boots seemed to like the kennel, maybe Annie would use it the next time she flew back to Texas for a visit.

When Annie slipped into her car, she pulled her cellphone out and dialed Ian. "Annie! Did everything go smoothly?"

"Yes," Annie said. "Boots went along with it suspiciously well. But I did learn something very interesting." She told him about the new locks on the kennel door and the strange behavior of the neighbor. "I wonder if he lost interest in complaining when the kennel turned out to be a more useful neighbor than he expected. And now that he's locked out again, he's using the complaining to access their logs."

"Well, it's not conclusive," Ian said, "but it is interesting. I don't suppose you found out how many animals were in the kennel? We might want to keep an eye on the other owners."

"Well, Isabelle Murkleson's Pomeranian is still there," Annie said. "And a bulldog that lives on a boat. Since the owners took the boat with them, I don't know who the burglar would rob with that information."

"So that leaves you," Ian said.

"Yes," she answered. "That leaves me. Do you think we should call off watching the kennel? Since I'm the only person who's going out of town in the kennel, we could focus on my house. Especially now that we know that no one could get into the kennel's back door at night anymore."

"We know that, but we can't be certain the burglar does," Ian said. "I think we don't have enough evidence to settle on this neighbor. We need to keep the plan in place and see where it takes us."

"OK, sounds good. I need to give Alice a call."

"Good. And Annie? Thank you for calling me right away."

"You worry too much," Annie said. "I'm sure nothing is going to happen to me. We'll catch this guy, get your sculpture back, and help everyone in Stony Point sleep a little easier."

"I hope you're right." Ian said as he hung up.

Annie looked down at the phone in her hand. She hoped so too.

— 14 —

When Annie called Alice, her friend agreed that they should stick with the original plan. "Do you think we should call Chief Edwards?" Alice asked.

"Ian didn't seem to think my experience this morning would impress the chief much. It is mostly supposition."

"But it makes sense," Alice said.

"Suspecting Jensen made sense too," Annie said. "And suspecting Isabelle Murkleson made sense. But they didn't turn out to be real leads. I think we need to stick with the plan. We could end up with something real to pass along to the chief."

"Whatever you think," Alice said.

"Are you feeling better today?" Annie asked tentatively. "You seemed stressed last night."

"I'm fine," Alice answered, but she didn't elaborate. Annie suspected she was about as fine as she'd been the night before. Whatever was bothering Alice, she clearly wasn't ready to talk about it.

The plans confirmed with Alice, Annie drove home to do a little yard work before beginning her "going out of town" act. She pulled weeds in the front flower beds and wandered through the yard, picking up sticks that had blown down. She loved the fact that a breeze blew all summer long, but it certainly meant she spent more time picking up sticks and branches than she ever had in Texas.

She was carrying a load to the compost bin when Ian pulled into the drive. Annie wondered what had brought him to the house.

"I thought I would give you a ride to the Jetport," he called loudly as he stepped out of the car.

Annie glanced down at her watch in surprise. It was later than she'd thought. She was surprised that she'd worked through lunch. At that thought, her stomach growled noisily. Since Ian had closed the distance between them quickly, he was close enough to hear the grumble, and he smiled. "I'll buy you some lunch on our way out of town," he half-shouted at her.

"Do you really think we're being watched?" she asked quietly.

Ian shrugged. "You never know."

"Well, come on inside so I can grab some empty luggage," she said with a smile.

Ian followed her into the house. Annie closed the door behind him quickly to keep Boots from rushing outside, and then she remembered that Boots was at the kennel. "I'm really not used to Boots being gone," she said.

"Think of it as Boots having a kitty spa day," Ian said, laughing.

Annie walked into the living room where she'd left a small pile of luggage. "That's practically true. There are almost no animals at the kennel to compete with her for attention. Apparently people are afraid to leave town—and afraid to leave their pets at the Freemans' business."

"Well, I hope we can do something about that." Ian

began picking up the pile of luggage. "Let me carry these out to the car."

"Are we really going to stop for lunch, or should I grab a snack for the car?" Annie asked. "I missed lunch."

"We'll stop by the diner," Ian said. "We can talk about your trip there and be sure it ends up common knowledge."

"Do you really think Grey Gables is likely to be a target?" Annie asked. "I still don't think it's nearly as grand as the other homes that have been targeted."

"I think we can sweeten the pot a little at the diner," Ian said.

"How?"

"Let's talk about another large portrait you 'discovered' in the attic and plan to have it appraised as soon as you get back from your trip," Ian said. "With the value of the portrait of Stella—that alone should be tempting enough. And that's not to mention the other Betsy Originals you have."

Annie nodded. Her grandmother's cross-stitch artwork had gathered quite a bit of fame, especially since her death. Annie had to admit, she'd been astounded at the worth set on the beautiful original cross-stitch portrait when she had it insured. "Yes, that might do it."

Before they left the house, she and Ian walked into every room, pulling curtains and blinds. It not only gave the house a more abandoned feel, it would also help hide Annie's return in a few hours.

By the time they reached the diner, Annie found her stomach was almost too nervous to be hungry. Peggy hurried to greet them when they walked through the diner door. "Annie!" she said cheerfully. "You look back to normal."

Annie smiled. "It was just a bad cold."

"You still looked a little pale when you were here with Alice and Jim," Peggy said. "Now you look all pink-cheeked and healthy again." Then she cut a teasing glance at Ian. "Unless it's Mr. Mayor putting roses in your cheeks."

"I do what I can," Ian said. He purposely raised his voice slightly. "Now I'm driving Annie to the Jetport in Portland, but I thought I'd better feed her first."

"Oh, right, Mary Beth told me about your trip," Peggy said with a wink.

Annie looked at her in mild surprise. She wondered who had told Mary Beth. She certainly hoped their secret plan wasn't completely common knowledge. A trap everyone was talking about wouldn't be much of a trap.

As Peggy hustled them to a table, Annie's eyes swept the diner. She jumped when she recognized one man, sipping coffee and glaring out the window at the street. It was Bryan Norman. Annie laid a hand on Ian's arm and nodded slightly toward the window.

Peggy seated them a few tables away from the window, poured them coffee, and took their order. As soon as she'd left, Annie whispered to Ian, "Do you know how Mary Beth learned of our plan?"

He nodded. "I told her. Well, technically, I told Kate. They would never forgive you if you closed them out of the loop, but I knew you had other things on your mind."

"They *would* be mad about being left out," Annie said. "But not all my dear friends are exactly known for their secret-keeping skills."

"I think they can manage to keep it within the loop for twenty-four hours," Ian said mildly as he sipped his coffee.

"Probably," Annie said.

"So," Ian said, allowing his deep voice to expand past their table. "Did you call the insurance company?"

"Not yet," Annie said, speaking up. "I didn't have time before this trip. I'm sure the portrait will be worth about the same as the last one."

"I don't like you leaving a valuable cross-stitch by your grandmother in your living room," Ian said. "Especially with the break-ins."

"I'm sure the thief wouldn't know a cross-stitch portrait could be worth so much," Annie said cheerfully. "I was certainly surprised when the first one was appraised."

"Betsy Originals are constantly increasing in price," Ian responded. "You really should get a security system. I don't like you living way out near the lighthouse at Grey Gables with no security system."

"Normally I have Boots," Annie said with a fake chuckle. "But she'll have to wait until I get back from my trip to take up her guard-cat duties."

When Peggy returned, she wished Annie a good trip. "Do you need me to go by your house and get the mail or anything?" Peggy asked.

"No, I had it taken care of," Annie said. "The house can look after itself until I get home."

"How long do you plan to stay in Texas?" Peggy asked.

"Just a couple days," Annie said.

Peggy smiled and winked again, and then turned back to waiting on her other customers. Annie picked at the grilled cheese that she'd ordered. Sitting so close to the man they suspected made her nerves even more edgy. She jumped when Ian's warm hand settled on hers.

"It's going to be OK," he said quietly.

"I hope so." Annie wanted Ian's sculpture back for him so much. And she wanted everyone in Stony Point to feel safe again.

After lunch, Ian drove Annie out of town and then looped around and came back into Stony Point from a different direction. Annie ducked down when they got close to her house, and Ian pulled his car far up the normally chained-off road that led to the lighthouse driveway. Then they quickly walked back down the gravel road and fastened the chain that blocked access before crossing to Alice's house. *Alice and Jim should be leaving soon to set up the stakeout at the kennel,* Annie thought, seeing the Mustang parked in the driveway.

She and Ian slipped through Alice's yard to creep back to Annie's house the back way. With all the windows covered, the house was almost gloomy inside. Annie shivered. It didn't feel like the same cozy home.

"Remember," Ian said, "this is just temporary."

Annie nodded. "Right, just until some horrible person breaks in."

Ian smiled. "It does sound bad when you put it that way. Are you having second thoughts? We don't have to do this."

Annie held up a hand. "No, this is the right thing to do. We need to find this guy before he can get rid of the things he's stolen."

"I'll be right here with you the whole time," Ian said.

"I know." And she did know. More than that, she knew how much it mattered to her.

— 15 —

Alice knew the strained silences that stretched between her and Jim were entirely her fault. She had no reason to be mad at him. She'd hoped he wouldn't propose, and he hadn't. And yet, with each passing day, she felt angrier about it. Why didn't he propose? Didn't he love her? She knew it was wrong to be angry with him. She was probably driving him crazy. But she simply didn't know what to do about it.

Summer in Maine meant that dusk held off as long as it could—some light lingered until almost nine o'clock. Jim had spent the day making calls and plans for his book project. He'd be leaving soon. He'd signed a contract, and he needed to make the trips and take the photos. Alice could go with him or stay behind and miss him. The choice was hers. She didn't like either option. In fact, she was having trouble liking anything at all—including herself.

"When do you think we should leave for the kennel?" she asked.

Jim messed with something on his computer, and then looked up. "Not until dark. We'll be too obvious in daylight, and we know the break-ins at the kennel must be at night anyway. There's just too much activity there during the day."

"Right," Alice said. She wandered to a window and

looked out toward Grey Gables. "I assume Annie and Ian are back."

"I know they are," Jim said. "I heard the mayor's car when he pulled up the gravel road across the street." He looked up and smiled at her. "I lost my legs, not my hearing."

"I didn't know if you'd noticed," Alice said. "You've been busy."

"Feeling neglected?" Jim closed the laptop and patted the sofa cushion beside him. "Come and sit with me, Red. I'll make sure you're not feeling neglected in the least."

Alice shook her head. "Thanks, but I'm too nervous. I've never been good at waiting."

"It's one of my better skills," Jim said.

"Oh? I've never noticed you being the sit-around type."

"I didn't say I like sitting around," Jim said. "Waiting is about finding ways to pass the time. I still say you should come sit with me. I'll show you some of those ways."

Alice felt a smile tug at the corner of her mouth. "I'm sure you would."

Jim shook his head ruefully. "If you don't want to while away the next couple hours with me, then maybe you should bake something or tinker with your business stuff. I've seen you lose yourself for hours in client files. What's got you so on edge right now?"

Alice looked at him and considered just spilling the whole thing. The problem was that she wasn't completely certain what the whole thing was. Was she mad at him for not proposing? Was she scared that he would, eventually? Or was she scared that he wouldn't, ever? Was she doubting his feelings for her?

"Alice," Jim said, heaving himself off the sofa and limping toward her. "You know you can tell me anything. What's bothering you?"

Alice swallowed, her mouth suddenly dry. "I just know how important this is to Annie. She feels responsible for Ian's break-in."

"But she's not."

"I know that," Alice said, turning back to the window. "And she probably knows it too—in her head. But logic and feelings don't always work together."

"At least in women," Jim said.

Alice looked sharply at him, but his crooked smile and sparkling eyes made it clear he was just teasing her. She looked over his face, thinking how familiar the laugh lines had become to her. She knew the exact tilt of his grin, the exact shade of his eyes. When she saw the blue of the crisp Maine sky, she always thought of Jim now. He mattered to her, and she'd been a shrew for days. She smiled slightly and kissed him quickly on the lips.

"What was that for?" he asked. "Not that I'm complaining."

"I just like your face," Alice said.

Jim laughed. "That is not something I hear very often."

"You'd better not," she said. "I don't want other women paying too much attention to your face."

Jim raised his eyebrows. "We're not back on that silly Murkleson woman are we?"

"No, we're not." Alice said. "So, would you like to play a few hands of cards to pass the time before we have to leave?"

"Strip poker?" Jim asked, jokingly.

"No."

"Spoilsport." Jim followed her into the kitchen for some cards and coffee as they waited for sunset.

Keeping busy did help the time to pass faster, though Alice still felt jumpy. She could tell Jim was trying to charm her out of her sharp mood, but she still found she couldn't completely relax around him. She knew he could tell, but he didn't ask her directly about it. She wasn't sure if he was being a great guy and giving her space, or if he was just afraid of how she might respond.

With the top down on the convertible, the drive to the kennel was warm and breezy. Alice had changed into dark clothes, though Jim was fine as he was. Most of his wardrobe was dark shirts, dark jackets, and dark jeans. "I wonder if I should be concerned that you don't have to change to skulk around in the dark," she said.

Jim grinned. "I thought you liked my clothes."

"I like *you*," Alice said. "Your clothes mostly just look … comfortable."

"And they are."

They pulled off the road out of sight of the kennel and walked the last bit in the rapidly fading twilight. The time between sunset and night on the coast was often startlingly short.

Jim nodded toward the outdoor dog runs. "You know, we could sit on the concrete pad in front of one of the sheds in those runs. We'd be completely in the shadows, but we'd also have a clear view of the door and all the back windows."

Alice nodded. "Sounds good. I'll follow you."

Jim picked the shed with the best view and carefully opened the chain-link gate to avoid rattling. "Watch for dog

… um … leavings," he said. "I don't think you want to ruin a pair of shoes tonight."

"Oh gross," Alice whispered. "How am I supposed to see dog poop in the dark?"

"The owners are pretty clean around here," Jim said. "They probably already scooped up everything."

Alice wished she'd found that more comforting than she did. She followed Jim into the run and tried to walk as lightly as possible. With every step, she dreaded a possible squish under her shoes. She reached the concrete pad at the back of the run without feeling like she'd stepped in poop.

Jim leaned against the shed that served as a dog-house when the animals were outside. The greater height helped pull the heat upward, away from the animals when they sought shelter inside from the sun. Jim and Alice wouldn't try going inside, the view was better from the shadows.

In order to stay in the shadowed overhang of the shed, Alice had to press close to Jim. He put an arm around her waist and whispered into her ear, "I'm beginning to really like this detective stuff."

"Don't get distracted," she whispered back.

"Too late."

"Jim Parker!" she whispered fiercely. "We're supposed to keep an eye on the door."

"I'm watching the door," he said. "But I have to do something to stay alert. This could be a long night."

Alice bit back a giggle as Jim's hand tickled along her rib cage. "If you keep that up, you're going to be in the dog-house—literally."

Jim ducked down and peered into the darkness of the shed. "Might be fun."

"You're incorrigible."

"I try."

Alice's glare was lost in the darkness, but she hoped Annie was having a better time keeping Ian focused than she was with Jim.

*　　*　　*　　*

Back at Grey Gables, Annie had no complaints about Ian's behavior as they sat side by side on the floor in the living room under the front windows. As always, he was kind and courteous. *Well,* Annie thought, *except when he's being bossy.* Sometimes his concern for her made him confuse advice with flatly telling her what to do.

Still, as they waited in the shadowy dark, she had no complaints about his behavior. She was extremely glad not to be waiting alone. "Does the chief have any ideas about when the break-ins usually happen?" Annie whispered.

She could barely make out Ian's head shake.

"We know from the night you rushed to my house that it was before three in the morning since that's when you called me," Ian said. "Had you been at the house long?"

Annie shook her head. "Maybe a half hour."

"So the break-in at my house was no later than three. That suggests we may see action here within the next couple of hours."

Suddenly Annie had a panicky thought. "You don't suppose the thief will have a gun?"

"I don't see why he would," Ian said. "He seems to take care to only break into empty homes. Besides, I'm not really planning to do more than identify him and call the police—well, text actually. I told Chief Edwards that he might be getting an important text from me tonight."

"And he didn't have a million questions?"

"I think the chief is getting used to our adventures," Ian said. "At any rate, you don't need to worry."

"That's good," Annie said. "Since I've had a gun pointed at me before, I can definitely say that's not something I'd like to see repeated."

Annie saw Ian's white teeth flash in the gloom. "You would probably be threatened less if you weren't quite so insatiably curious."

"Is that some nice way of calling me nosy?" Annie asked.

"No. You care too much about others to be nosy. Nosy is just looking for entertainment from the suffering of others. You actually want to make things better."

"Not everyone looks on my curiosity so kindly," Annie said.

Ian took her hand in his. "The people who really matter figure it out eventually."

Annie leaned back against the wall, thinking that she was having an amazingly good time considering she was sitting on the floor in the dark waiting for her house to be broken into.

The night was still and warm. They'd run out of things to talk about, so they sat in silence. Annie's eyes strained in the gloom, looking for any sign of movement. Once or twice, she was almost certain a shadow had shifted in the darkness, but when nothing more happened, she realized she was just trying too hard.

Time takes on odd shapes and speed when you're sitting in the darkness. Annie felt sleepiness nibbling at the edges of her concentration, but her tense nerves kept it from making any real progress. She wasn't certain how long they sat still and quiet. It might have been just minutes or hours. Time felt that way, as if it couldn't be counted and measured.

Then she heard something and every nerve in her body tensed. Ian laid a quieting hand on her arm, but she could feel the tension humming in his muscles as well. Was it finally time?

There was another soft sound—shuffling with a bit of squeak at the end. Ian eased himself away from Annie and stood, moving away from the soft light of the window and into the deeper shadows near the doorway that led into the hall. Annie followed close behind him, though not so close as to make him trip if he should need to suddenly reverse direction.

The sound of movement grew clearer as they reached the hall. Someone was in the house.

Ian paused. He turned to Annie and mimed talking into a phone. Then he pointed for her to move farther from the doorway where the light from the phone wouldn't be seen. She didn't like moving away from him. *What if the burglar comes down the hallway?* she thought. *What if he has a weapon?*

Still, she needed to text Chief Edwards. She well knew that. She slipped through the darkness; her familiarity with the room made her passage silent. In the darkest corner of the living room, well away from the doorway, she pulled out her phone. As hard as it was to resist the urge to keep her eyes on the living room doorway, she purposefully turned her back to help hide the glow of the phone. She shielded the screen still more with her hand. She picked Chief Edwards's number from her speed dial and sent the message that their trap was sprung and the burglar was in Grey Gables.

Before she could put the phone back in her pocket, it vibrated with a new text message. It was from the chief: "Get out of the house."

"Ian is with me," Annie typed back.

"Both of you. Get out of the house."

"I'll get Ian. Come quickly," Annie typed feverishly on the tiny keyboard. She wouldn't leave the house without Ian, and she wasn't certain he would leave without catching the burglar. For all that he talked about staying safe, she knew how much he wanted this man caught.

Annie turned back toward the living room doorway. It was empty. Ian had gone after the burglar. Annie felt a surge of worry as she crossed the living room again to follow.

She slipped into the dark hallway and began walking slowly toward the kitchen. She heard a yell and a sudden crash of furniture. Ian had clearly confronted the crook. Annie threw off all attempts at stealth and ran down the hallway toward the kitchen.

She nearly stumbled when she heard another crash from her rarely used dining room. Annie stepped through the doorway and saw two shadowy figures fighting. Annie knew one must be Ian, but since the two men were nearly matched in height, there wasn't enough light to make out which one was which. She groped for the light switch and flipped it on.

The flood of light made her blink, but she could see Ian struggling to wrestle Bryan Norman to the ground. The intruder was slightly stockier, and it looked like the weight advantage was working against Ian. Finally the burglar threw Ian off and raced for the doorway, directly at Annie!

Annie jumped back out of the doorway. When Bryan Norman charged through, she slammed hard into him from behind. The combination of his momentum and Annie's added weight kept the man from making the turn up the hallway. Instead he slammed head-on into the opposite wall.

He stumbled back, shaking his head, and Ian tackled him. This time, the stockier man fell to the floor.

"Annie," Ian called from on top of the squirming man's back, "do you have any duct tape?"

"In the kitchen," she said, edging around them to reach the kitchen.

"Please hurry," Ian said as Bryan Norman bucked hard, nearly unseating him.

Annie grabbed the duct tape from the junk drawer, and Ian quickly taped the burglar's hands behind his back. Then while Ian remained seated on the man, Annie taped his ankles together.

"Now that's a nice bit of hog-tying," Ian said as he climbed off the intruder.

Annie grinned. "I didn't think I would ever get to say this, but this isn't my first rodeo."

Ian was still laughing when they heard the siren in the distance. The police were on their way.

~ 16 ~

The next day, Annie was the center of attention at the Hook and Needle Club meeting. Peggy didn't even bother to pull out her quilting project. She just sat at the edge of her chair and peppered Annie with questions. "I can't believe you had all this excitement without us!" she said.

"It was a little more exciting than I expected," Annie said. "I would have cheerfully missed that part."

"But Ian was so brave," Peggy said. "That's very romantic."

Alice laughed. "It is a little less romantic when I picture Ian sitting on the burglar's back, pleading for duct tape."

"You say that because you had your own romantic night with your own handsome pirate," Peggy said, "cuddled up in the dark."

"In a dog run," Alice said. "All I could think about was the possibility of dog droppings on my good shoes."

Everyone turned toward Stella when the elderly woman cleared her throat pointedly. Her knitting needles never paused during the meeting, and they made tiny clicking noises as she looked at Annie. "Romantic heroes aside, did the villain confess to all the burglaries?"

"Eventually," Annie said. "Bryan Norman was still shouting that he was going to file assault charges against everyone when the chief hauled him away. But Ian told me this morning that he cracked when they found all the stolen merchandise in his garage."

"All of it?" Alice asked.

Annie felt her eyes grow wet as she nodded. "Even Ian's sculpture. Apparently Ian will have to wait until after the trial to recover it though. All the stolen goods are evidence now. Oh, and Ian solved the mystery of why the man looked familiar to me. Apparently, he was one of the people eavesdropping at the church when Ian was telling the chief about Vanessa's auction discovery, which means we now know why the auction ended so suddenly."

"Well, I know I'll sleep better at night," Kate said, "knowing the guy is behind bars."

"I bet the kennel owners will be happy too," Alice said. "No more complaints."

Annie doubted the happy part had soaked in yet. "Actually, I expect they feel horrible, knowing the crook was using their client list to pick victims."

"That certainly isn't something you could put on your promotional material," Gwen said dryly. "So does that mean the chief was wrong about the culprit 'casing' the properties first?"

Annie shook her head. "Apparently the information Bryan Norman got from the kennel just pointed him in the right direction. He still had to check out each property, which he did by doing plumbing work for at least one of the owners. It seems Mr. Norman was a retired plumber. He worked on a leak in the Dunhams' laundry room. Apparently he was good at talking his way into people's lives. Or in the case of the kennel— yelling his way in."

"And what exactly was his motive?" Stella asked.

"The chief thinks he initially just wanted bad attention to be cast on the Freemans and the kennel," Annie explained. "After a break-in or two he apparently thought it was just an easy way to pad his retirement funds. He thought he would just sit on all of the goods for quite a while and then sell them when the heat was off. In the meantime, he figured he would have put the kennel out of business."

"Speaking of the kennel," Alice said, "have you picked up Boots yet?"

Annie shook her head. "I'm going to get her after this meeting. I didn't think it would be a good idea to bring her home and then leave her right away. I don't know how upset she's going to be."

"I probably wouldn't expect any cuddles today," Alice said.

"Unless Mr. Mayor comes by," Peggy teased.

Annie felt her face warm up at the teasing. "I'm sure Ian will be busy today after all of this excitement. He didn't get a lot done yesterday, that's for sure."

"And I'm sure we'll never see the day when Ian doesn't have time for you," Kate said. "You know, I admit when Alice first told us about the break-ins, I thought it was the young man who works at the kennel—the one who can pick locks. I think maybe I am not as fair-minded as I thought."

"Well, he was our prime suspect for a while," Alice said. "It was Jim who didn't think the kid was a thief."

"Still, it's made me think," Kate said. "You know Vanessa has stayed in touch with Logan Lariby. And I've not been thrilled. He's an actor, and I look at young actors as bad influences. Even though Logan has been nothing but polite, I've hung onto that feeling."

"You just want to keep Vanessa safe," Mary Beth said gently.

"I do," Kate said. "But am I being fair? I wouldn't have wanted her to be friends with someone like that boy at the kennel either. And he turned out to be a fine young man who's just doing his best to help his family. I realized I've got to stop viewing every boy with so much suspicion. My feelings about Logan haven't really been a great thing for my relationship with Vanessa."

"Well, it's never too late to change," Mary Beth said.

"And to give yourself a break," Gwen added. "I know all about jumping to bad conclusions about your child's ... friends."

Everyone turned sympathetic glances toward Gwen. She'd come close to ruining her relationship with her son by her distrust and dislike of his fiancée. Now, of course, she loved her new daughter-in-law dearly.

"Of course," Kate said. "I'd like it best if Vanessa didn't get interested in any particular boy until she's about thirty, but I'm definitely going to schedule that trip to the city to see Logan's play. At least I'll be able to do it without picturing my house being robbed now."

"Which brings us back to our victory cheer," Mary Beth said. "Yea for Annie and Alice!"

"And Ian," Annie said. "And Jim."

"How much longer is Jim going to be in town?" Peggy asked.

"I'm not sure," Alice said, her voice almost leaden. "He's going to need to leave soon to start his next project."

"Is this the one where you can go with him?" Mary Beth asked, eyeing Alice curiously. Annie noticed that everyone's attention had sharpened at Alice's tone. Clearly, whatever was bothering Alice for the last couple days was still bothering her.

"He's going to be traveling all over the world this time," Alice said. "I don't expect I'll be seeing much of him for quite a while."

"So you made your decision," Annie said.

Alice smiled, though the look wasn't very cheerful. "I guess."

"Have you talked with him about it?" Annie asked.

Alice looked around her at all the avid attention. "It's not a big deal. Traveling is key to his work. He's always going to do it. He's not exactly the kind of guy you get serious with."

Mary Beth crossed her arms and gave Alice a doubtful look. "Except when you do."

"The heart wants what the heart wants," Peggy added.

"Look, my life isn't a greeting card," Alice said. "Nor is it some romantic comedy. Sometimes there's no good answer. I like Jim. A lot. But his job, his life, his nature—they just don't really mesh with mine."

"He makes you happy," Annie said quietly.

Alice turned a flat look toward her. "Do I look happy?"

"No, but is it Jim's fault? Or is it something you're doing to yourself?"

"I appreciate you all," Alice said. "Really. But there's a

reason why it's called a private life. It's because it works best when it's kept private." She turned her wrist to look pointedly at her watch. "And I'm going to need to run. I have an appointment. It was fun, and I'm glad the bad guy is in jail. See everyone next week."

Everyone stared in surprise as Alice stood and hurried out the door.

"Wow," Gwen said. "I assume there's trouble in paradise?"

Annie's gaze stayed on the closed shop door. "I don't know what's going on with her. I suspect we won't find out until she sorts it out for herself."

"Do you think I should apologize?" Peggy asked. "I didn't mean to upset her."

Stella turned a stern look toward Peggy. "Now, don't go blaming yourself. Whatever Alice is so touchy about, she brought it in with her. You didn't do anything wrong."

Peggy looked gratefully at Stella. "Still, I should probably go too. I don't want to be late getting back for the lunch rush."

Everyone made consoling comments, but it was clear that Peggy still felt bad when she left. "I do believe this is the most depressing victory meeting I've ever been to," Gwen said. "But I want to tell you again, Annie, I really appreciate you sticking with this mystery. Even though John and I don't have any pets to put in the kennel, I'm still going to rest easier knowing the burglaries are over."

"I think we all will," Annie said.

The meeting wrapped up soon after Peggy left. Mary Beth promised everyone that next week would be totally focused on actual Hook and Needle Club business. "I have some ideas for the summer craft fair," she said as everyone stood to leave. "So I'd love it if everyone would come next week ready to talk about that."

"Talk about needlecrafts in a needlecraft club?" Gwen said wryly. "How novel."

"I'll find it refreshing," Stella said as she slipped her neatly folded knitting back into her bag.

"Oh, you can't fool us," Mary Beth said. "All this mystery stuff has grown on you too, Stella."

"All things in moderation," Stella said sternly, but Annie caught a slight quirking of the corner of her mouth. Stella was just playing matriarch again. In reality, she loved the pull of a mystery now and then. "If we have another mystery thrust upon us," Stella added, "it would be nice if we could all play more of a part in solving it."

"Oh?" Annie said, giving the older woman a fond smile. "Did you want to go to pawn shops with me?"

A look of horror crossed Stella's face. "Of course not!"

"You also missed out on the visit to the young man's trailer," Annie said. "I washed dishes and picked up used tissues."

Stella's face wrinkled in disgust. "Perhaps we could have a nice sanitary mystery next time."

Mary Beth burst out laughing. "I'm sure Annie will do the best she can."

Annie was still smiling when she walked out of A Stitch in Time. She was surprised to see Alice leaning on the side of her convertible, clearly lost in thought. Annie walked over to her friend.

"Are you OK?"

Alice looked up, surprised. "Oh Annie, is the meeting over already?"

"It wasn't much fun once you left," Annie teased.

"I wasn't exactly the life of the party."

Annie leaned against the side of the car next to Alice. "I know you said you wanted to keep your private life private, but I hate to see you unhappy. Don't you think you should try *talking* to Jim?"

"And tell him what?" Alice said.

"How you feel."

"What if I don't know how I feel?"

"Then tell him you're confused. And that you love him. You do love him, don't you?"

Alice nodded.

"Is he back at the house?" Annie asked.

Alice shook her head. "He's at the diner. I was supposed to join him for lunch after the meeting. He has to leave in the morning for New York. I don't want him to leave with things so up in the air. He's being patient with me, which is only driving me more crazy."

Annie smiled. "You should probably go face the music. You know there's one thing I absolutely know from having been very happily married."

"What's that?" Alice asked.

"There's nothing more important than honest communication," Annie said. "Even when you have to honestly admit how conflicted you are."

Alice nodded. "Well, I'll try a page out of the Annie Dawson handbook then. Wish me luck."

Annie hugged her friend. "You don't need luck. You both have something better. You love each other."

Alice gave a wry snort. "And love conquers all."

"If you let it."

— 17 —

When Alice walked into the diner, the smell of comfort food enveloped her like a hug. Her gaze swept the room until she saw Jim waiting for her. He caught her eye and smiled. It was the smile he always wore when he saw her, full of mischief and affection.

Peggy spoke to her hesitantly, her eyes anxious, "Do you want to join Jim, or do you need your own table?"

"I'll join Jim," Alice said. Before Peggy could rush away, Alice caught her arm. "I'm sorry. I was horrible at the meeting."

Peggy's smile was like seeing the sun break through rain clouds. "No problem. I'll get you some coffee."

"Thanks."

Alice took a deep breath and walked across the room. She slipped into the chair across from Jim.

"Did you have a good meeting?" he asked.

Alice nodded. "Everyone is very relieved to have the crook in custody. Stony Point isn't the kind of town where we're used to being scared to leave our homes."

Jim looked around the room. "Yeah, this is a nice place."

Peggy hurried over and filled Alice's cup. "Are you ready to order, or do you need some time?"

"Soup," Alice said. "You can surprise me about which kind. All your soup is great."

Peggy's smile squinched her eyes nearly closed. "One surprise soup. And you?"

"Give me the same. I trust Alice's judgment."

Peggy nodded and rushed away while Alice looked at Jim, wondering if there was some message hidden in his order.

"You know what I've been thinking about?" he asked.

Alice shook her head.

"My first visit to Stony Point. The first time I saw you, you took my breath away."

Alice raised an eyebrow skeptically. Jim laughed. "I'm not kidding. You were beautiful and happy and adventurous. And I never thought you'd be interested in someone like me."

"Sure you didn't," Alice said, raising her cup for a sip. "That's why you flirted with every woman in Stony Point."

Jim chuckled. "That's habit." He looked down into his cup. "You know, I noticed you were jealous of Annie back then. You didn't like me flirting with her. That's when I thought, just a little, that I might have a chance with you."

"I just never could compete with Annie," Alice said. "She's been gorgeous since she was a kid. And sweet. It was hard to hate her for being beautiful when she was such a fantastic friend."

"You don't need to compete with anyone," Jim said. "Annie's a lovely lady, but you—you're a force of nature."

Alice smiled. "Like a cold rain?"

"More like a hurricane," Jim said. He reached out and took her hand. "I need to go tomorrow. I don't know when I'll get back. I wish you'd tell me what's going on with you before I go. I don't want to leave when things aren't good between us."

Alice looked down at Jim's large hand over hers. His knuckles were scarred and one finger was a little crooked as if it had once been broken and hadn't quite healed right. "Things are fine," she said.

Jim sighed. "Sure they are."

They sat in silence, each sipping coffee. Alice felt the pressure of all her conflicted feelings building up in her like lava waiting to burst from a volcano. She didn't know what to say. She felt fragile, as if she could break something—something she didn't want to do without.

"You know," Jim said, setting his cup back down on the table, "I did a photo essay for a magazine a few years ago on wild horses. They're amazing creatures. They can be totally confident and strong—and scared—all at the same time. I went out every day to photograph this one small herd. And they got used to me, sort of."

Alice looked at him over the rim of her cup. Jim was a storyteller, always launching into one tale or another. She wondered if he was trying to smooth things over with this story—to bring their relationship back to normal. She appreciated the effort. "Sounds amazing."

He nodded. "One day, one of the horses was feeling more curious than scared, I guess. She walked right up to me, just out of reach. We looked at each other for a long moment. Then she chuffed at me and raced away. I left the next day. I had to get the photos processed and the essay submitted, but I still have that moment—that perfect moment of being right there with this wild, beautiful creature who wanted to be with me ... just for that moment."

Alice tensed slightly, waiting for the message in the story.

"Ever since I met you, I've been waiting for the time you'd run away," he said. "I know a woman like you ... well, I knew you couldn't stay interested in someone like me—someone who is only half a man—for too long. And I don't want to hang on when you want to run. You can tell me, Alice. It's OK. If you want me to stay away, you can tell me."

Alice looked at him in amazement. "Is that what you think is going on?"

He shrugged. "I don't have a lot of illusions. I'm too old for them and too beat up. I knew you were out of my league the second I laid eyes on you. But every second we've been together has been amazing."

Alice continued to stare at him in disbelief. "You're kind of an idiot," she said finally.

Jim's eyes widened in surprise. "Well, I didn't quite expect that."

"Jim Parker, I love you," Alice said. "I'm not the kind of person who just gets tired of the man she loves."

"Then you tell me why you've been pushing me away since I got here this time," he said. "Look, you can be honest with me. You can just tell me that being with a guy with no legs is a little more than you want to sign on for."

"You think I have a problem with your legs?"

"Of course," Jim said, his voice rising. "How could you not have a problem?" He stopped when people at the surrounding tables turned curious eyes toward them, and then he lowered his voice again. "Look, I know there are amputee groupies. I've met a couple. And I know full well that you aren't one of them."

"Right, I'm not an amputee groupie," Alice said. "My love is for *you*—with legs or without. Don't you know what being with you has done for me? My ex sucked every bit of confidence out of me. He was a lying, cheating con man. I thought that's the best I could get. I came back to Stony Point, and I felt lost. Friends helped. They helped a lot, but it was *you* who made me feel beautiful and special."

"You *are* beautiful and special," Jim said. "And fiery and stubborn and really challenging. I love you, Red. I'll love you until the day I die."

"Then why didn't you ask me to marry you?" The words came out of Alice's mouth before she could stop them. She felt them hanging in the air between them.

Jim's face filled with shock and wonder. "You wanted me to ask you to marry me?"

"Yes," Alice said. "No. I don't know. I don't know what I want. I'm scared. I'm scared of losing you. I'm scared of losing this fantastic, heart-pounding adventure we're on. And I'm scared of losing my safe place in Stony Point. Our lives don't fit together at all, but the thought of not being with you makes me so miserable I can't stand being around myself."

"Alice MacFarlane, I would marry you in a hot New York minute," Jim said. "I'd marry you and spend the rest of my life making sure you didn't regret marrying a ruffian like me. I didn't ask, because I didn't want to scare you off. If what we've had since the day I met you was the most commitment you were comfortable with, I was willing to adapt to that."

Alice felt her eyes fill as she looked at him.

"Alice, every second that I'm not with you, I'm missing you," he said. "I love my work. I love what I do. I love my life. But every time I have to leave Stony Point without you, I feel like I'm leaving a vital organ behind. I can feel it missing in my chest like a cold, hollow spot."

Alice looked at him in wonder. Jim was always so quick with a teasing quip or a good-natured bit of flirting. He made their relationship seem so easy. "I didn't know you felt like that," she whispered.

"I know that rat you were married to kicked your heart around pretty bad," Jim said. He squeezed her hand. "You know, I'm not that much better. Before the explosion that took my legs, I was a heartless womanizer. It was so easy. But then, between one moment and the next, everything changed. I looked down at the flat blankets in the hospital, and I knew … I just knew no woman would ever want to be with me again. And I was right for a long time."

He looked down into his mostly empty coffee cup. "I still flirted and charmed. I met a few women who seemed interested until they found out my limp wasn't just a bum knee. You, though … you never acted like you even noticed I was only half a man."

"You aren't half a man," Alice said. "You're the man I love."

Jim grinned. "So do you want me to propose? I will. I'll even come as close as I can to getting down on one knee. You might have to help me back up, but I'll give it a try for you."

Alice shook her head. "No. I don't think The Cup & Saucer is ready for that. I think we're good."

"So, do you want to go on a world tour of the most romantic cities in the world?" he asked.

Alice's smile turned sad. "I don't know. I don't think so. A year away from here? A year away from my business and my house? I have house payments."

Jim smiled. "That's not a problem. I have money saved up. I wouldn't let you lose your house."

"And I want to pay my own bills," Alice said. "I want to know I can take care of myself before I consider letting someone else take care of me."

"Well," Jim said, "if you're my assistant, I could pay you. Then it wouldn't be me giving you money. It would be work. You're a *very* good assistant—quiet and obedient."

"Right," Alice said.

"How about we do this?" Jim said. "You come with me tomorrow to New York, and we take each city as they come. Be with me when you want. Be here when you want. One step at a time."

"I could do that," she said quietly.

They both jumped when Peggy showed up with their soup. "I'm sorry," she said. "I didn't mean to interrupt."

"That's OK," Jim said. "We have lots of time to talk. All the time we need."

Alice nodded, her heart feeling lighter than it had in many days. "All the time we need."